The Panacea Doctor

The Panacea Doctor

The mysterious disappearance of a beloved physician

Andrew I. Schafer

Copyright © 2025 Andrew I. Schafer.

All rights reserved. No part of this book may be used or reproduced by any means, graphic, electronic, or mechanical, including photocopying, recording, taping or by any information storage retrieval system without the written permission of the author except in the case of brief quotations embodied in critical articles and reviews.

Archway Publishing books may be ordered through booksellers or by contacting:

Archway Publishing
1663 Liberty Drive
Bloomington, IN 47403
www.archwaypublishing.com
844-669-3957

Because of the dynamic nature of the Internet, any web addresses or links contained in this book may have changed since publication and may no longer be valid. The views expressed in this work are solely those of the author and do not necessarily reflect the views of the publisher, and the publisher hereby disclaims any responsibility for them.

Any people depicted in stock imagery provided by Getty Images are models, and such images are being used for illustrative purposes only. Certain stock imagery © Getty Images.

ISBN: 978-1-6657-6536-7 (sc)
ISBN: 978-1-6657-7479-6 (hc)
ISBN: 978-1-6657-6537-4 (e)

Library of Congress Control Number: 2025905048

Print information available on the last page.

Archway Publishing rev. date: 6/27/2025

*To my extraordinary family:
my wonderful wife Pauline;
children Eric, Pamela and Kate;
grandchildren Nathaniel, Caroline,
Evan, Samantha, Patrick, Meghan;
and in-laws Melissa, John and Sean,
my gratitude for putting up with me.*

Cast of Characters

Nick Wolff, immigrated with parents from England

Lili and Stephen Wolff: Nick's parents

Dr. Ernest Peltz, the doctor

Ludwig Krüger, mathematician from Germany

> Wife, Gertrude

> Sons Herbert "Bert," age thirty-five, US Coast Guard officer

> Hermann, age thirty, FSU chemistry professor, and Max, age twenty-eight, lawyer

Martha (Kitchens) Langston, mother of Jimmy and stepmother of Gunner Elkins

Otis Langston, husband of Martha, KKK member

Jimmy Langston, Nick's friend

Hunter Langston, Jimmy's half brother

Jim Morton, Martha's fiancé

Mrs. Louisa Peacock, Martha's sister in Tallahassee, living with Jimmy

David Moran, assistant professor, criminology, FSU

Dr. Rachel Moran, wife of David, a gynecologist at TMH

Hannah Spielman, Dr. Peltz's first wife; assistant to Dr. Gisella Perl at Mount Sinai

Dr. Harold Alexander Abramson, Mount Sinai allergist/pediatrician

Sidney Gottlieb, recruited Dr. Peltz for MKUltra

Dr. Gisella Perl, survivor of Auschwitz, infertility specialist at Mount Sinai (1951–79)

Dr. Houston Calhoun, staff physician at Tallahassee Memorial Hospital

Dr. Michael Stanton, young doctor, graduate of Mercer University, recruited by Dr. Peltz to join his practice

Paul Adams, FBI first contact in the investigation

Michael Scarpano, FBI agent

Steve Whiteside, FBI agent

Mrs. Feldman, busybody Jewish lady at the seder

Stewart Bradshaw, MD, pathologist who did the autopsy

Rebecca, Rachel Moran's twin sister

Courtroom:

Judge Graham Rutledge

Travis Dawson, bailiff

Drew Griffin, lead prosecutor

Holden Cunningham, lead defense attorney

Chase Aiken, junior defense attorney

Prologue

The man and a boy were winding up a productive morning shore fishing off the pure, soft sands of Alligator Point's secluded beach. Their bucket of seawater was filled with the fish they landed—redfish, speckled trout, grouper. It was an unseasonably hot April day, and the blaring sun was starting to bake the Gulf Coast of the Florida panhandle. The boy's attention was caught by a large, dark mass far down on the beach, and he tugged on the man's T-shirt.

"Look, Pa," he said excitedly pointing to the blob.

"Ain't nuthin' but a beached whale," the man said shrugging his shoulder.

"Don't bay funny. There ain't no whales in the Gulf."

"There sure is them. Sperm whale, blue whale, humpbacks."

As the man started to pick up the fishing gear, the rods and reels, tackle box, bait, knives, the bucket for catches, and all, the boy ran off toward the object.

From far away he shouted back, hands cupped around his mouth, "Pa, Pa, this ain't no whale."

When the man got there, he saw a hideously bloated and

decomposed body facedown in the sand. He told his son to run off with all the gear, put everything in the truck, and stay there.

The grotesque face of the corpse was unrecognizable. Aside from a shredded shirt, he had no clothes on, and his mud-covered and massively swollen body was covered with deep lacerations, abrasions, and all kinds of other wounds. His sloughing skin was darkly discolored and wrinkled. A yellowish-brown waxy material coated large patches of his skin. One hand was jaggedly amputated. And the stench emanating from the drowned corpse indicated that putrefaction had begun.

The man ran back to his truck and drove the boy home quickly. Then he drove off to the Wakulla County Sheriff's Office in Crawfordville, up north about twenty-five miles toward Tallahassee on US 98, to report what he had found. The sheriff's assistant knew right away that something important must have happened because the face of the man looking at him was frozen in a state of horror. The sheriff said he knew whose body it was. The year was 1964.

1

Arrival in Purgatory

Stepping off the overly air-conditioned Greyhound bus, Nick Wolff hit what felt like a wall of scorching heat and dense humidity, something he had never experienced in England. The soles of his shoes got stuck in the goop of melting tar on the recently paved outdoor bus station. It was August 1959. Nick was twelve years old. He had just arrived in his future home, Tallahassee, Florida, population 48,174. An old city bus took him from the bus station to 1113 Buckingham Drive, a single-story, redbrick ranch house with a low roofline, where his parents met him. They had moved here a few weeks earlier, and Nick had stayed behind with distant relatives in Newark, New Jersey, after disembarking in New York from the ship that took them here from England, passing the Statue of Liberty.

Nick had spent his boyhood in London. He was prepared for the alien environment into which he was deposited. Yet he now felt strangely unperturbed, filled only with great expectations.

Nick was enrolled in the laboratory school of Florida State

University (FSU), located at the periphery of the campus. One of his first friends was an older boy named Jimmy Langston. They met and bonded over their passion for soccer, a fringe sport in America at the time. They went to pickup games played by mostly international FSU students on a poorly maintained soccer field. The goal posts lacked nets, and the boys would sit to watch on overgrown grass along the sidelines. Eventually they were grudgingly invited to play when a team was short on players or when substitutes were needed.

Nick and Jimmy had another interest in common. While living in England, Nick had become an ardent reader of murder mysteries. He had read almost all the fifty-six Sherlock Holmes short stories by Arthur Conan Doyle, as well as his four novels. He had devoured many of the Agatha Christie murder mysteries that featured detective Hercule Poirot. His new friend told Nick that he was not particularly fond of reading, but he was a huge fan of spy movies. Nick and Jimmy skipped school one day and went together to the Florida movie theater for the matinee opening of the first James Bond movie, *Dr. No*. Whenever a murder or kidnapping was reported in the *Tallahassee Democrat*, the two of them, a young Poirot and a young Bond, would chat about possible perpetrators and motives.

Nick found out that Jimmy lived with his aunt in Tallahassee. He soon realized that Jimmy didn't want to talk much about his family. He'd just gotten his driver's license, so his aunt, Ms. Louisa Peacock, let him use her second car, a 1960 Plymouth Valiant. Jimmy drove Nick all over town and its outskirts. Nick was especially struck by a neighborhood called Frenchtown, where apparently only Negroes lived. Lined along dirt roads, he saw nothing but dilapidated wooden shacks, older folks on their porches in rocking chairs and the younger ones running around in groups, in rags or half-naked, along with stray chickens and dogs. Nick had never seen anything like this in his life, but he was curious.

"I'll tell you more about all this later," Jimmy said, "but what we have here is hard-line segregation of races in every part of life. You know, Nick, these people are descendants of slaves ... and many of our own descendants were slave owners."

Nick was fascinated. He didn't read about this in English history books.

"That's why you don't see any Negroes in our school, Nick, except for some of the caretakers like toothless old Joe Washington," said Jimmy.

"Will it be always like this?"

"*No!*" replied Jimmy. "God, no!"

"How do you know that, Jimmy?"

"There is some stirring around the country to desegregate. Desegregate both public places, schools, and eventually neighborhoods, I suppose."

Nick stayed silent.

"You know what?" Jimmy continued. "My parents say this is where they should stay, as these folk like it this way. They have their families and friends so close by, so they must be happy. But I ask myself how anybody could be happy living like this."

On February 13, 1960, six months after Nick's arrival in Tallahassee, students at Florida A&M University, the college for Negroes in the city, and Negro high school students staged a sit-in at Tallahassee's downtown Woolworth's store lunch counter, where a large directive was posted to the effect that Negroes were not allowed to sit there. The sit-ins were repeated every two or three weeks, each time accompanied by an increasingly menacing police presence with warrants for arrests. Jimmy convinced Nick to join him in supporting the Negroes. Nick never asked his parents for permission. At noon on March 12, the boys steeled themselves as together they entered Woolworth's, but all the luncheon stools were already occupied by mostly Negro men and a few Whites. The customers were sitting, and the servers momentarily stopped talking to look at the boys and then quickly turned back to whatever they had been doing. So the boys just stood behind them in solidarity. Policemen charged with enforcing segregation entered and forcibly escorted or dragged all those sitting at the counter, Negro or White, out of the store under arrest for unlawful assembly. They pushed them into paddy wagons that would take them to the Leon County Jail.[1]

Back at school, the chatter among the students was how Jimmy and another boy were seen taking sides with the Negroes. There were no repercussions for Nick, as most of the students didn't even know him yet. But for Jimmy, well, *he* was ostracized and shunned by much of the student body and expelled from the prestigious Key Club to which he had only recently been elected.

2

Into the Forest

On a late Saturday morning in September 1960, when the weather was still unbearably hot, Jimmy and Nick set out on a road trip to the house of Jimmy's parents down in Panacea. They drove past faded billboards, dilapidated, ramshackle cabins, a rusty school bus by the side of the road, and tiny churches in much disrepair. Getting onto Highway 98 South, about halfway to the Gulf Coast, the scenery changed strikingly. They entered a seemingly eternal stretch of dense forest, with towering pine trees, evergreens, turkey oaks, and cypress shading the highway from both sides. The wind blowing through the car's open windows swept in the aroma of pine resin, magnolias, and later down the highway, the salty smell of ocean breezes from the approaching Gulf's warm waters that tends to hang thick in the air on days like this.

"Appalachian National Forest," said Jimmy, pointing left and right. "In there you can easily get lost and find many old cypress swamps. There are even snakes, possums, bears, and gators."

"Gators?"

"Yeah, alligators. Watch out. They sometimes crawl across the road here."

By now, it was sunset. They passed a road sign: "ENTERING PANACEA. Pop. 920."[2]

"Does that mean a population of nine hundred twenty? Christ!" Nick said as Jimmy took a sharp left onto a dirt road that passed deep through the forest. He slowed down as the car was being jolted by bumps and rocks. They arrived at a large clearing.

"What are all those caravans?" Nick asked.

"Caravans?" Jimmy replied. "You must mean *trailers*, don't you? They're called *trailers* here."

The "trailer park" accommodated about ten or so vehicles, randomly arrayed. Parked in a corner of the clearing were old cars and small trucks. They got out into the still blinding sun and heat of the late afternoon, with wind gusts signaling an approaching rainstorm.

"Who lives here?" Nick wondered.

"Only poor people ... and *this*, Nick, is where *I* grew up!" Jimmy exclaimed in a mock tone of bombast, with an arm outstretched toward it. In front of his family's trailer was a rusted metal porch glider, one of those that just screeches back and forth when people sit in it and move it, like a horizontal swing. There were also a couple of aluminum beach chairs as well as an outdoor grill with a likewise rusted dome-shaped lid.

Up a couple of wooden steps, Jimmy opened the unlocked door to his parents' trailer. Inside it was starkly dark in contrast to the still glaring sun outside, but it wasn't a lot cooler. A prevailing smell of stale cigarette smoke lingered within the trailer.

"Hey, Mom," he called out. A woman kneeling to clean the oven stood up and came over to hug him.

"Jimmy, Ah didn't know yawl wuz coming over today, or else ah would'ave prepared something. And who is this boy?" The woman turned to Nick and shook hands with him.

"It's a pleasure to meet you, Mrs. Langston." Nick bowed slightly and smiled. "My name is Nick ... Nick Wolff." He immediately became acutely self-conscious of his posh English accent and was embarrassed by it.

"Wha, Ahm Martha Langston. Welcome," she said. "Why you speak so charmingly. Are yawl sum kinduh foreigner?"

"Yes, ma'am. I just came from England."

"How *cute*!" she exclaimed delightedly with a gravelly voice. "Come on in and set down at thuh table. Do yawl want sumpn to drink? And ah have sum leftover pie if yawl hungry."

"Thanks, Mom. Can we have some soda and a piece of your delicious pecan pie?" Jimmy asked.

"Oh yes, that would be scrumptious," Nick added, as Mrs. Langston started to giggle.

As Nick's eyes accommodated to the dark, and Martha turned on the light around the dining table, he was struck by how attractive Jimmy's mother was. Dirty blond hair, deeply bronze tanned complexion, shapely in cut-off denim shorts, and with a glowing smile. Only later did he see in the daylight that her skin was weather-beaten, leathery, and wrinkled on her face, and when she smiled, crow's feet formed at the outer edges of her eyes, no doubt partly caused by constantly smoking cigarettes.

Nick looked around the cramped trailer. There was no separation between the kitchen, dining table, and living area, and only a flimsy curtain hid what must have been the sleeping area and bathroom in the back. The appliances and furniture looked well worn. Yet Nick was struck by the trailer's immaculate cleanliness and the absence of clutter.

Jimmy's half brother, about whom Jimmy had told Nick about, came in. His name was Hunter Langston, born to his father's first wife. He looked quite a bit older than Jimmy. Hunter muttered something inaudible. He didn't even acknowledge Nick's presence. He sat at the table, taciturn and silent. Nick introduced himself but couldn't engage Hunter in conversation. Jimmy broke the silence.

"Hunter works for a doctor nearby, over in Panacea. The doc has developed a good reputation since he arrived in these parts. His name is Dr. Peltz, and he goes over to his Panacea office every morning from his home in Apalachicola. It's an amazing house. I'll have to show it to you sometime."

"What kinds of work, Hunter?" Nick asked, turning toward him.

Only Jimmy responded. "He does odd jobs for the doctor in both places, his home and his office, and serves like a caretaker for his house since the doctor lives there alone. Gets well paid, don't you Hunter?"

Again, there was no response, and Nick was beginning to think Hunter was dim-witted.

Jimmy and Nick were about to leave when Jimmy's father, Otis Langston, burst through the door. He was tall, unshaven, with a beer belly that was partly revealed under his soiled, sleeveless T-shirt, obviously in a foul mood from the start. Ignoring the boys, he directed his wrath at Mrs. Langston.

"Goddamn it, Martha, you never cleaned out my truck like I told you to. What the f***ing use are you, woman?" He shouted in a thundering, raspy voice, sputtering spits of saliva.

"Ah wuz gunna do it, but yawl had taken it away—" Martha started.

"Shut up, you stupid bitch," he yelled. As he approached

the boys, still shouting at Martha, he was reeking with the stink of stale alcohol and tobacco.

Nick was stunned and wasn't about to say anything that could only make the situation worse. But when Otis threw the remains of the pie on the floor, flinging the plate at the wall and barely missing Martha, Jimmy firmly grabbed his father's arm and asked him to go outside for a talk. When they returned, Otis appeared to have calmed down a bit, and he even silently nodded toward Nick. He staggered to the room behind the curtain and shouted, "I'm late! I gotta go!"

"Would you like some dinner, Otis?" Martha asked. There was no response.

He emerged from behind the curtain carrying over his forearm some kind of folded white clothing and lurched toward the door, fumbled for the knob, and then slammed it behind him.

While his silent half brother remained motionless, Jimmy went over to his mother and embraced her as she tried everything in her power to avoid crying in front of her guest. It was clear to Nick though that her boys had seen this before many times.

"He's going to his usual meeting, and you know how riled up he always gets before going there," Jimmy said to his mother.

3

The Langston Family

On the way back to Tallahassee, Jimmy talked about life with his parents. What Nick had seen was why Jimmy was now living with his aunt, Martha's sister. Jimmy said, "A couple of years earlier, my mother had decided that she could no longer abide seeing me grow up in such a degenerate environment. Martha herself had dropped out of school in sixth grade and was basically uneducated, mostly illiterate, and certainly not cultured or refined."

Nick now heard from his friend that Martha's classmates in elementary school, many years ago, sometimes provoked her by calling her "trailer trash." And as an adult, Martha not infrequently saw better-dressed people in the street in conversation, turning toward her and even pointing at her as she overheard them muttering "White trash" or "trailer trash."[3]

But Martha was also a kind, innately street-smart, and strong woman. She wanted her son to thrive in high school with the best teachers and good, sensible friends, and then go on to a fine college after which the world would be his oyster, as she often told him, far away from her own wretched life.

On their way back to Tallahassee, Jimmy driving, Nick heard about how Martha met Otis in 1945 when he came home from the war in the Pacific, traumatized by his experience there. Nick remained silent as he listened to his friend recounting the story of his parents. They both lived in Crawfordville at the time, a few miles north, so it was easy for them to cross paths. Before Otis went off to war, he was married to another woman, and they had Hunter. Not long after Otis left to join the military, his wife moved with Hunter to Pensacola. There she met an older, wealthy businessman. After a brief courtship, if there was any such at all, she filed for divorce from Otis, placed Hunter in a foster home, and ran off with her new husband to whereabouts unknown. She did leave notes for Otis and his parents, giving them the name, location, and contact information for the foster home where Hunter was placed, as well as the legally transacted permanency plan for children with the foster home. She didn't inform Otis about that. As soon as he came home from fighting in the war, Otis drove to Pensacola to pick up Hunter. He then found out about his first wife's infidelity.

Jimmy continued with the sad story of his parents, just as he had heard it in pieces from his mother, Martha. Soon after meeting Otis in Crawfordville, Martha became pregnant with Jimmy, and she and Otis married later in the year. But Otis was a damaged man. At first, Martha worked hard to support him in his constantly moody and depressed state. She helped him go to sleep at night when he couldn't do it himself and reassured him when he awoke with nightmares. She would try to talk him out of his negative thoughts about himself and offer her hand during his periods of feeling hopeless about the future. However, he became increasingly irritable and volatile, starting to have aggressive outbursts.

At the same time, he distanced himself from his sons and old friends.

As Jimmy told Nick, nothing Martha did seemed to stop Otis's personal deterioration. He took to drinking heavily starting in the mornings, to which he later added amphetamines and barbiturates. He became increasingly abusive toward Martha when he was intoxicated, which was most of the time, and started to throw objects at her. Then the beatings began, even in front of their crying boys. At the same time, Otis was increasingly expressing virulent and hateful thoughts about Blacks, Asians, Jews, immigrants, homosexuals, socialists, and practically anyone who was not of his race and religion.

As the 1954 civil rights movement gained momentum throughout the country following the Supreme Court's decision striking down segregation in public schools through the *Brown v. Board of Education* case, and then the Civil Rights Act of 1957, the dormant decades of an organized Ku Klux Klan saw a major resurgence in response to what the Klansmen and their kin saw as a threat to their old ways of life. In some regions of the Deep South, including North Florida, the Klan became particularly active, carrying out violent acts, including flogging, mutilation, and lynching, night riding with cross burnings, and overt intimidation and even assault of the ones they considered undesirable. They had parades of strength in Klan regalia. So it wasn't long before Otis, now unemployed, became radicalized and an easy target for recruitment.

To try to appease Otis, Martha joined the Women of the Ku Klux Klan, the WKKK, originally an auxiliary organization linked to the KKK. By 1950, women were allowed to formally join the Klan. While women in the Klan rarely participated in violent acts, they formed social clubs regionally centered around a shared ideology of racism, xenophobia, and bigotry. They actively crusaded for White supremacy, organized social events, and went to rallies with their husbands or boyfriends. Martha didn't do this reluctantly as she herself was raised in a Klan family. Her father was a prominent Kleagle[4] in the 1920s when the KKK was at the height of its power with about five million members nationwide. With time, Martha's conversations with anyone, even strangers, became peppered with racist comments and derogatory descriptions of those the Klan persecuted.

4

Dr. Ernest Peltz

Nick's father had a chronic heart condition, and he was looking for a well-qualified internist or cardiologist to follow him in what was then a limited group of doctors practicing in Tallahassee. One of his young faculty colleagues in FSU's Criminology Department, David Moran, had found one for himself at the recommendation of his wife, Rachel, a gynecologist who had become very familiar with the medical community in the area. He was a German Jewish physician named Ernest Peltz, probably in his midsixties, who David thought was outstanding. Professor Stephen Wolff talked about this at dinner one evening with his wife, Lili, and Nick. The only problem was that Dr. Peltz practiced in Panacea, a thirty-minute drive from Tallahassee. He did have evening office hours on Wednesdays, however. Since Nick now knew where Panacea was, he offered to accompany his father after school one afternoon.

They easily found the one-story brick building in Panacea, with a large sign brightly lit up: "Ernest Peltz, Dr. med."

The office was modest but had a large, tastefully furnished

waiting room and a well-equipped examination room. Dr. Peltz came out of his office to the front door when the bell rang. He was a short, pudgy man with a red face and a double chin, wearing a white shirt with a colorful bow tie, his trademark, as Stephen had been told. He walked with a distinct limp of his left leg. To make it less noticeable and embarrassing at certain times, he used a cane held in his opposing right hand for support. When seeing patients, he put on an impeccably clean, well ironed, and starched white coat that was always a bit too large for him, its sleeves extending down to his knuckles when he was upright. He wore flat circular glasses with thin iron rims that saddled the bridge of his nose, the old-fashioned type that flashed reflected light on whoever was facing him just by the wearer's slightest head movement. Dr. Peltz also had a missing middle finger on his left hand, amputated below the middle knuckle, leaving a stump. He was self-conscious about it, but since he was right-handed, he was able to mostly hide it by keeping his left hand loosely clenched. He told Stephen and Nick that he didn't like people asking about it, but when pressed he said it was a childhood accident and nothing more. As for the limp, he told those who asked that he was born with clubfoot on the left side that caused that foot to be permanently pointing down and turned inward and, as a result, his left leg was shorter than his right one.

Dr. Peltz was indeed a genial man who spoke English fluently but with a strong German accent. Since his next patient had canceled her appointment, he brought Professor Wolff and Nick into his office for introductions.

"I got my medical doctorate from the University of Göttingen," he started. "As a Jew from an observant family, we saw the dark clouds gathering over Germany as far as back as 1935 when the Nüremberg Laws were enacted. You know what—"

Nick's father interrupted. "Sadly, I do know, Dr. Peltz. Jews stripped of citizenship, denied admission to universities, forbidden to intermarry with non-Jews, and such. Similar things that were also happening at the same time in Hungary when I was trying to starting my law career."

"So you are a lawyer?" Dr. Peltz asked.

"Not anymore," Nick's father responded. "Law is not like medicine, you know. If you want to practice law in another country, you must essentially start all over again. Every country has its own legal system, but the practice of medicine is universal. So I ... reinvented myself, I guess you would call it, as a sociologist, and took a faculty position in criminology at FSU when we came to Tallahassee."

"I see," said Dr. Peltz. "It must have been a traumatic transition."

"Not really. My wife and I had survived far more trauma during the Holocaust."

"We should talk more about that later because I suspect it may relate somehow to your heart problem," Dr. Peltz replied. "As I was saying, I had just finished my medical training, now finding myself without prospects for a decent career in Germany as Hitler assumed power. When Kristallnacht[5] occurred in November 1938, it was the last straw for me. My family had some relatives in New York to sponsor me ... and so I came to America, alone. My foolish parents, may God bless their souls, insisted on staying behind, and they perished in the concentration camps."

"So did you already have a position arranged for you when you arrived in the States?"

"Ha-ha!" Dr. Peltz exclaimed with irony as he tilted back in his squeaking wood swivel chair, hands clasped behind his head. "Not at all. Until I could find a proper job, I reluctantly agreed to be a resident in training in internal medicine at the Brooklyn Naval Hospital and then at the Long Island College Hospital, earning a minimum wage. Hardly what you would call world-renowned medical centers. But they did provide me with useful experiences in taking care of very sick, complicated patients, learning the American medical system, and polishing my English."

"So that must have prepared you well."

"Oh yes," Dr. Peltz replied. "I was able to secure a loan to open a practice on Park Avenue, among some of the wealthiest residents of Manhattan—old money, as they say. I worked my behind off, offering office hours six days a week including evenings. Things went well ... very well, at least financially. After several years, with a large base of patients, I was able to get an appointment at Mount Sinai Hospital to do medical research for part of the time, which I had always enjoyed greatly in Germany."

"So why would you move here of all places? It was a curious move on your part," asked Nick's father.

"That's complicated, Professor Wolff. I was married in New York to a nice, well-educated Jewish woman, and we used to take vacations in this area of the Gulf Coast. We loved the serenity and even talked about retiring here one day. But then my wife died suddenly. A stroke. A great tragedy. But now, finally having some financial security, I could come here earlier by myself as a widower, just a couple of years ago."

"But not to retire ... clearly," Nick's father said.

"I am what do you call it in English ... a workaholic! So now let's get on with why you are here tonight. We'll go into the examination room, and young Nick here can sit in the waiting room. I will turn on the TV for you," he said as he faced the boy.

With a lot of available time that evening, Dr. Ernest Peltz wistfully talked to Stephen Wolff about how he prepared for his move from New York by purchasing a magnificent but abandoned, rundown pre-Civil War mansion in Apalachicola, overlooking the beach and the Gulf. Dr. Peltz proudly described his two-story structure, atop a small hill, with some steps leading up to the large front door, which was flanked by Greek Revival columns. A back door led to the garden and down to the dock and beach. Covered porches wrapped around the ground floor, and the second story likewise had a wraparound balcony. Inside the door was a grand vestibule with two spacious winding staircases to the upper floor. The mansion was in a state of dire neglect when he bought it, even exhibiting considerable external damage caused by hurricanes and a fire in the 1940s. But Dr. Peltz engaged a local historic preservationist to hire workers who would restore the building to its former glory. When Dr. Peltz moved in, he took on a gardener to create gardens that would surround the house, populated by neatly organized native flowers of the Deep South.

"Townsfolk and others from the local area regularly came to watch the renovation of the mansion," said Dr. Peltz. Rumors began to circulate about a distinguished physician from New York who would be moving in there. A German, and what's more a Jew. When Dr. Peltz finally arrived by himself, he heard that there was some local chatter about why he would need such a large house, living alone.

Dr. Peltz quickly endeared himself to many of his neighbors, although some did express concern and displeasure with the presence of a rich Jewish doctor, a German no less, moving from New York into this peaceful neighborhood. He hosted lavish catered Sunday brunches for the residents of Apalachicola and Panacea, with personal invitations to selected groups of them at a time. On these occasions he also gave the people brief tours of the house.

His reputation as a brilliant, hardworking, thoughtful, and compassionate doctor spread fast, all the way to Tallahassee, especially in view of the dearth of reputable physicians who had been available previously. Nevertheless, he was told in no uncertain terms that he would not be allowed to see Negro patients. Dr. Peltz openly expressed his strong disapproval, but at least for now, he didn't want to alienate the local population.

Even Martha and Otis became his patients after he was recommended to them by their son Hunter, who was already working for Dr. Peltz. An old log cabin sat on the edge of a forest, looking down onto the Gulf shore, but also within sight of the doctor's big house. Dr. Peltz had it completely restored inside and out, and even upgraded it, to serve as Hunter's home, enabling him to keep an eye on his mansion whenever the kind doctor was away.

Dr. Peltz was eager to integrate himself into the medical community, joining the Leon County Medical Society and gaining privileges at the small Tallahassee Memorial Hospital, off Miccosukee Road. He was also warmly accepted by the small but growing Jewish community in Tallahassee, maybe just forty or fifty families in 1958. Even before moving here, Dr. Peltz had contacted Rabbi David Eichorn of the new Temple Israel on Mahan Drive to ask to join the Tallahassee Jewish congregation. Dr. Peltz was initially warmly welcomed and became a generous donor. He drove up on Friday evenings for Shabbat services as often as he could, coming directly from seeing patients in his Panacea office, dressed in a dark suit and wearing his yarmulka even though most of the others were more informally attired. In recent years the congregation became invigorated by young Jewish FSU faculty members, like David and Rachel Moran, as well as a growing number of enthusiastic Jewish students at FSU. Dr. Peltz told everyone how delighted he was to see this whole new generation of Jews.

But the local prohibition on seeing Negro patients in his office ate away at him. To any official who would listen, he vented his anger at the pervasive racism enforced here. To them, he likened it to the kind of institutionalized antisemitism he lived with in Germany. But his grievance was simply dismissed. Dr. Peltz finally decided to purchase a simple ranch house in the Negro section of Panacea, had some of the walls demolished, and converted the spacious house into a modern medical office not unlike the one he already had. To placate the community, he hung a sign next to the front door: "ERNEST PELTZ, M.D., MEDICAL OFFICE, **COLORED ONLY**." The last two words were in bold letters in the custom of that time in the South. Likewise, on the signage to his original office in Panacea, he added "**WHITES ONLY**." So by the end of 1958, during his first year practicing in the area, both offices were operating. Dr. Peltz hired two nurses, one a White woman and the other a Negro, each to staff his two offices and to cover for him while he was working at the other site. The distance between the two offices was only a ten-minute walk, making it easy for him to go back and forth.

If anything, Dr. Peltz went out of his way to be even more attentive and gracious to the Negro patients than his White ones. As an added benefit to his Negro patients only, he created a small pharmacy in the Colored Only building where he was able to supply his indigent patients with some free medications.

5

Point of No Return

Close to midnight on a stormy Saturday in the winter of 1960, insistent knocking at the front door awakened Dr. Peltz in his home. He put on his gown and hurried downstairs. He hadn't heard the doorbell ring because the noise of the thunderstorm had drowned it out. He put on all the lights, looked through the front window and saw a woman and a boy standing there, drenched but now under the shelter of the second-floor balcony. He cautiously opened the door and there was Martha Langston with her son, Jimmy. As Martha parted her soaked hair, he recognized her; he had seen her once as a patient for her liver problem.

"My God!" Dr. Peltz exclaimed. "What happened to you, my dear?"

Martha was sobbing so hard she couldn't speak. So, Jimmy, who had driven down from Tallahassee after his mother called him, took over. "He beat her again, worse than ever," he said.

Martha knew that Dr. Peltz had heard from Hunter

Langston something about his and Jimmy's parents constantly having fights whenever Otis drank himself into a blind rage.

"Come in; come in," said Dr. Peltz. "Let me look at you in the light." Martha's breathing was shallow and painful. She had an extensive bruise around her right eye. She was pressing a soaked handkerchief to the back of her neck, under which the doctor saw a deep laceration that was still bleeding. There were smaller lacerations over the right arm that were clearly fresh.

"He cut her with a broken bottle," said Jimmy.

"I am afraid the only decent hospital in this area is all the way up in Tallahassee," bemoaned Dr. Peltz. "So let's take you to my office in Panacea and see what we can do."

Jimmy and Martha sat in the back seat as the doctor drove as fast as he could through the driving rain and gale-force wind. Hunter had been nowhere to be seen. Visibility was difficult, but thankfully the roads were deserted. The car was parked right in front of the entrance to the clinic. They had forgotten to bring umbrellas, so they quickly scurried through the door that Dr. Peltz unlocked. At his Panacea clinic, Dr. Peltz flipped on all the lights and took Martha with her son to the examination room, where a surgery room light hung over the table.

"Martha, please lie flat on your stomach on this table," Dr. Peltz instructed.

Dr. Peltz then adjusted the surgical light from the ceiling to focus on the back of Martha's neck. After scrubbing his hands and putting on sterile surgical gloves, Dr. Peltz cleaned the area around the laceration with iodine swabs. He then injected lidocaine around the cut and told Martha not to move. A suture kit had been opened and prepared next to the table, as well as some other sterile instruments. Dr. Peltz gently probed the wound itself to make sure no broken glass was in it. Then, despite his missing finger, he deftly sutured the laceration within just a few minutes. Gauze was taped over it. He examined the other wounds and decided they didn't need to be sutured, just sterilized.

Suspecting a broken rib, he prepared to do a chest X-ray. The examination room was equipped with an old portable X-ray machine, and Dr. Peltz had learned how to take a radiogram and how to develop the film. There were three fractured lower ribs on the right side. So Dr. Peltz skillfully applied an elastic compression wrap around the lower chest. Back at his home in Apalachicola, he gave Martha an opioid analgesic, wary of her history of substance abuse.

The storm was still raging outside.

"You are not going home now!" he said to Martha in a commanding tone. "Both you and Jimmy can use two of the vacant bedrooms in the back of the ground floor. The beds and pillows are made, and you can use a large bathroom nearby with privacy."

"Jimmy," he said turning toward the boy. "I understand you live in Tallahassee with your aunt. But it would be a dangerous drive back there tonight, so you can have the other bedroom. Let's all try to get some sleep, and we can talk in the morning."

Dr. Peltz was accustomed to sleeping late on weekends, but he woke up early to the unaccustomed aroma of fresh coffee. As he came down the stairs in his gown, he heard a sizzling sound coming from the kitchen. Martha was there, making omelets with eggs she found in the refrigerator and brewing coffee.

6

Unwanted Visitors

Jimmy was already in the living room. In the clarity of daylight, with Martha feeling better despite her ripening black eye, it was time to discuss what might be best for her moving forward. Jimmy wanted to be part of the conversation before he drove back to Tallahassee.

"Martha," Dr. Peltz began, "I don't know you well, and I know your husband, Otis, even less, so pardon me for my presumptuousness if this is intruding on your personal lives. I am speaking with you now not just as your doctor but as someone who might be able to give you some thoughtful advice, ... having experienced quite a bit of trauma in my own life."

"Doctor, you've been so kind," Martha replied haltingly. "Ah don't mind at all. Even if ah don't know that word y'all just said. Presump ... something.

Dr. Peltz smiled warmly. "Being presumptuous means being audacious or bold."

After some silence, he continued. "It's my personal opinion that you shouldn't go back to live with Otis at least for the time being. Only worse things can happen."

"Y'all have no idea how often I've gone through this. He usually apologizes," said Martha.

"I am sure he does," continued Dr. Peltz, "but no sooner, it would happen all over again and again. And maybe more painful each time. I know he has not been well mentally, but that's not a good enough excuse to be abusive, which I regret to say he appears to have been to you for years."

"Listen to him, Mom," Jimmy said, leaning forward in his chair toward her. "He's right, you know. I never want to see you get hurt like this again."

Martha was now holding back tears.

"But what am ah to do now? Where can ah go? Ah can't ask my sister in Tallahassee to do me another favor and let me live there like you," said Martha facing Jimmy. "And even if ah could, I wouldn't be able to stay out of your way, Jimmy. And the whole reason for having you live up there was to keep yawl away from that godawful home yawl had been growin' up in."

The doorbell rang, and Dr. Peltz unsteadily got to his feet with the assistance of his cane to see who it was. It was Hunter. He had noticed the lights on in the house during the night and came to see if there was a problem.

The rain was still coming down through the stiflingly humid air. "Dr. Peltz," Hunter muttered with his head bowed, "where is my stepmum?"

The doctor waved Hunter over to where they were all sitting, brought him a cup of coffee, and gave him a recap of last night's events. He told Hunter that they were in the middle of discussing what his stepmother should do now.

Dr. Peltz turned back to Martha. "I think you should stay here for now. You can have the privacy of your own accommodations, exclusively, and without fear. And, of course, the rest of the house whenever you want to change scenery."

"Oh no, Doctor," Martha said, "ah can't possibly impose on you like that, 'specially after what you dun for me already."

"Auch der Lieber!" Peltz blurted out in German, looking up at the ceiling in exasperation. "Oh heavens! But you see you wouldn't be imposing at all. I have a plan. When I ate that delicious omelet you made this morning, I thought to myself how wonderful it would be to employ you as a live-in cook and housekeeper. Light work, lots of time to do other things you might enjoy, a generous salary with free lodgings. I was planning to look for someone like that anyway."

"Ah gist can't believe how nice you are, sir," Martha said, somewhat startled. But both Jimmy and Hunter were smiling and vigorously nodding toward her, urging her to agree.

"And more," Dr. Peltz continued. "I will bring you to my office in Panacea on some days to show you how to be a good receptionist in a medical office. The one I have now is very nice but frankly inadequate. You would get to meet interesting people and learn a skill that you'll value in the future."

"And how should ah deal with Otis? Ahm dead scared of him now," she replied.

"On a day and at a time he is most likely to be not in the trailer—"

"Well, that's easy," Martha interrupted. "He spends all evening every night drankin' and smokin' and God knows what else he does with his friends. And yawl know hay goes to them Klan meetings regularly, and those are long f****ng meetings; ahv gone with him several times."

"You go there to that trailer when he is out and quickly pack all your belongings that you will need here. Hunter can accompany you. All right with you, Hunter?" Dr. Peltz asked.

Hunter just nodded silently, morose as always.

"You will write a note for Otis, Martha, which we can compose together this morning, simply stating the plain truth. That you took a nice job with me to be a live-in housekeeper and a paid part-time office receptionist."

"But he can't read mostly," said Martha.

"Don't worry about that. He'll figure it out and, if he must, he'll get one of his more literate friends to help him. Just leave the note on the kitchen table where he will be sure to find it, ... and don't do that until just before you are ready to leave the trailer with your belongings."

As Martha looked around the house in daylight, she saw that it was tastefully filled with cheerful, contemporary furniture, brightly painted walls decorated with colorful pictures, and beautifully polished hardwood floors of the type she had never seen before, partly covered by Persian rugs.

Dr. Peltz told Martha about the one room in the house that always had to have a locked door. He reassured her that nothing was secret in there, and, to appease her inevitable curiosity, gave her one chance to look inside with him. It was Dr. Peltz's private study where he spent most of his time in solitude whenever he was at home. The study was unlike anything else in the house, a throwback to a past era in prewar Germany. All four walls supported floor-to-ceiling bookshelves, filled with old medical books he had brought down from New York. There was an antique, rolling library ladder made of oak with wheels attached to it to enable him to reach books stacked on the higher shelves. In one corner stood a plush, comfortable vintage armchair next to an ornate floor lamp that emitted soft, shaded lighting. The eccentricity of this room was highlighted by the oddly heavy dark burgundy window drapes that were always kept closed. The whole study was permeated by the musty smell of old library books. This was where Dr. Peltz spent his evenings, smoking a pipe and reading when he was not sitting at his large, period piece desk.

"I'm so assured, to see having Hunter nearby in his log cabin," Martha said.

"Hunter does seem to have a small group of, how would you say it, rowdy friends who visit him frequently and make a lot of noise," replied Dr. Peltz, "especially when they are drinking on weekends. But I don't mind; you know, I was like that at his age.

Dr. Peltz then told them that he sometimes woke up in the middle of the night hearing them, but he didn't want to meddle. He would just go right back to sleep.

Dr. Peltz gave Martha a blank check and told her to drive her old pickup truck to Tallahassee to Lerner Stores on North Monroe and buy some nicer clothes she can try on and pick out. Later, Dr. Peltz took Martha's beaten-up truck to the Muldon Ford dealership in downtown Pensacola, the most reputable in the panhandle, and drove back home in a used but well-maintained blue 1955 Ford Thunderbird that he bought for Martha.

On a Sunday morning in February 1961, Dr. Peltz awoke late and limped downstairs, as always holding onto the banister to pick up the local newspaper. Opening the front door, he was alarmed to see a big black Nazi swastika spray-painted on the porch. Another one was on the door. Taped next to the one on the door was a piece of paper. Nervously he read what was scribbled on it:

Pelts [sic]. Your holding a richous Christian woman in ther and raping her. Leave NOW, you f***ing Jew. We will get you if you don't.

His heart now racing rapidly and hands shaking, he dialed the Franklin County Sheriff's Office to report the vandalism and the threatening note.

Deputy Sheriff Jack Dolson answered, heard his complaint, and then told him to calm down. They were only some pranksters having fun.

Dr. Peltz exploded. "That's not fun! It's a serious matter, dammit. My life is being threatened," he said, uncharacteristically raising his voice. "I want this investigated immediately!" That last word, harshened by his thick German accent, was intimidating enough for the deputy sheriff to hang up on him.

Within a few minutes, three police cars, sirens blaring and spinning red lights flashing, screeched to a halt in front of the Peltz house. Martha and Hunter ran over while Dr. Peltz was already at the door.

Four officers with wide-brim, straw-colored Stetson hats with badges attached to them, dressed in khaki shirts and darker brown pants, came running up the steps to the house. They wore wide leather belts with large, decorative buckles around their waists, guns in holsters. All wore sunglasses.

Dr. Peltz opened the door, and one of the men stepped forward, standing legs apart. He ever-so-slightly tipped the front of his hat's brim.

"I'm Sheriff Moore, and these men behind me are my deputies," he said.

"Well, let me show you—" Dr. Peltz started, but the sheriff interrupted him.

"Just you hold your horses," Moore stated firmly. "Before you go any further, you must know the rules here. You don't give commands to our officers. It's the other way around; you see, the officers give *you* commands. Understand?"

"But I have to tell you—" Dr. Peltz started again.

"*Verstehst du?*" The sheriff now bellowed, crossing his muscular arms across his chest and removing his shades. "*Mache ich mich klar?* Am I making myself clear, ... sir?"

"Ah, you speak German," said Dr. Peltz, surprised.

"Patton's Third Army. I fought at the Battle of the Bulge, freeing those countries from you German bastards."

Dr. Peltz now knew this would be a difficult matter. "I understand," he declared.

"OK. Now let's see that notice you found on the door."

Dr. Peltz handed it to the sheriff, who read it slowly several times. Abruptly, he turned to his deputies, who were several paces behind him outside the open door, and said "you gentlemen need to step inside the door here and stand right behind me, hands on your guns. We got a bigger problem here!"

Dr. Peltz invited the men into the living room to sit and have some iced tea. But they didn't budge.

"Now it says here," Sheriff Moore began, "that you abducted a White Christian woman and have been raping her here in your house."

"Just a second," snapped Martha angrily, having just appeared and stepping to the front to face the sheriff. "That thar letter can only be referring to me 'cause no other women has ever lived here with the doctor."

Before Sheriff Moore could continue, Martha raised her hand to stop him. "Ahm not finished! Nuthin' in that paper could be farther from the f . . .ing truth. This *gentleman*, and that's what he is, yawl, offered me uh salaried position to work as a live-in caretaker for this large house. We sleep in different parts uh thuh house. Way nevur had no kinduh romantic interest in each other, and he has nevur evun so much as touched me. Ah swear to that on the Bible. He's a famous doctor, and he couldn't have ever even harmed nobody in his life." Martha was all riled up, red in the face.

"Well, we may have to pick that up when there are legal proceedings," said the sheriff.

"Aint never *gonna* be no proceedings," Martha shouted, enraged.

"All right, sweetie pie, calm yourself down. We'll see what happens. We got other matters we have to attend to now."

As the officers started down the steps to the front lawn, Dr. Peltz shouted after them.

"Hey, what about the swastikas?"

The sheriff stopped for a second and turned his head back. "I've seen swastikas before; no need to see any more."

"But I am being threatened because I am Jewish, as you saw," Dr. Peltz shouted.

The sheriff now turned fully to face Dr. Peltz directly and said, "Yeah. Ah never take threats lightly. You shouldn't either. And, by the way, you have quite a house here. Our regular folks around here can come and look at how wealthy, greedy Jews hoard money to be rich like you, and then them Jews have the balls to show it off."

7

Fire

When things settled down after the visit by the sheriff and his men, Martha spoke about it to Dr. Peltz.

"I've got uh confession to make, Doctor. Ah never did think good of Jews, though Ah'm not even sure if I ever saw one before you. Folks around here talk about them as murdering Christian children, jist as thay had done to Jesus, and smear their blood on the bread they eat at ceremonies. And then ah heard thay wanna take over thuh whole world."

"Did you ever hear of the Holocaust, Martha?" Dr. Peltz asked.

She had to think a bit.

"Yeah, ah think so. I heard that it never happened. They just spread the rumor about it."

Dr. Peltz sighed deeply. "Well, Martha, sometime in the future I hope I can be able to help guide you to the truth."

"Ah never meant to offend you, Doctor, ... of all people. You've already shown me that a Jewish person like you can be completely different from all that I learned."

Martha settled into her new roles well and seemed happy, at least satisfied. She unexpectedly turned out to be a fast learner in Dr. Peltz's office, proving to be an efficient receptionist. Because of this, Dr. Peltz convinced her to take adult education classes to learn basic skills like reading, writing, mathematics, and English language, and maybe to eventually take the GED exam for a high school diploma. The Wakulla County Adult Education classes were held in a community center in Crawfordville, a short drive for her from the doctor's office in Panacea. The tuition cost was nominal, but Dr. Peltz wanted her to pay for it herself from her salary. Martha had the sensitivity to understand that he was tacitly doing this to encourage her independence.

Martha's small class consisted of foreigners—two Asians, two Mexicans, and others from South America, Eastern Europe, and Africa. No Negroes were allowed. All her classmates were young, relatively indigent people who were struggling for upward mobility in society. She readily befriended most of them even though she had never in the past interacted with foreigners. She even organized lunches for them before classes at the brand-new Hardee's in Crawfordville.

Martha observed that Dr. Peltz continued to try to assimilate among well-educated people in the area, especially physicians at Tallahassee Memorial Hospital and faculty members at FSU. Like he had done with local citizens when he first moved to the panhandle, he would now invite small groups of these new acquaintances with their spouses to his home in Apalachicola for Sunday brunches that were deliciously prepared by Martha. At the beginning, Martha would just listen to the conversations, too self-conscious to speak because of her lack of language skills or knowledge of current world events. But she was eager to soak it all in. Only months later would she be confident enough to actively participate.

Dr. Peltz now sufficiently trusted Martha to talk to her in the evenings about how his day went and what he did. Martha observed that he didn't come home until late in the evenings on Fridays. He told Martha that he drove quite frequently to Tallahassee, not only for Friday evening Shabbat services but also to Leon County Medical Society events and lectures. He himself was later invited to speak to the other physicians on various medical topics of his own areas of expertise. Martha also knew that he occasionally flew back to New York, telling her that he had to be there to wrap up some medical research projects at Mount Sinai Hospital. When he came back on Sunday nights, Martha looked forward to hearing about his research projects. From what little he told her, she was fascinated.

Martha got to know many of his friends and colleagues who were invited to Dr. Peltz's home where they could exercise their devotion to fishing as a pastime. They talked about it a lot, comparing best fishing sites and equipment while boasting about recent big catches. Dr. Peltz later confided to Martha that he himself wasn't at all interested in fishing and, in fact, had never even been in a small boat. He asked Martha if she thought citing seasickness and his clubfoot were sufficient excuses to not join them. Dr. Peltz did eventually buy a lovely fishing boat. It was a Chris-Craft fourteen-foot, high-powered leisure boat made of fiberglass and red cedar, easily accommodating five people on faux leather seats. There was a dock right below his mansion where he or his guests could securely tie the motorboat. Although Dr. Peltz never used it and never even joined his guests on their trips, just having access to the swanky, custom-made boat itself became an attractive enticement for guests to Dr. Peltz's home.

Martha, however, learned how to operate the motorboat.

She learned how to start it, how to use the throttle, and how to steer it and trim it. She knew now that she could capably release the boat from the dock, removing all the lines that secured it. And she learned how to dock the boat on return and tie it up back onto its post. Martha loved making short sailing trips by herself around the Gulf. In the oppressive heat and humidity of summer, the brisk breezes that she sailed into provided better refreshment than anything else. And she made sure she would never get lost in the Gulf. She took an evening class on how to navigate a small boat. The boat was already equipped with compasses, marine and coastal charts of the Gulf, and parallel rulers and dividers.

Ironically, despite his aversion to boating, Dr. Peltz was proud of and even bragged about his long-distance swimming prowess. In fact, he had come close to winning a medal at the 1936 Olympic Games in Berlin in the fifteen-hundred-meter freestyle event, which involves thirty laps of a pool, almost one mile.[6] After the war, he resumed his rigorous training regimen. Moving into his new mansion in Apalachicola, he would devote at least an hour to swimming in the Gulf of Mexico, even if it had to be at night.

Dr. Peltz's excellent reputation continued to spread throughout the region, and his practice was booming. He participated actively in social networking during the limited hours he had available. An interesting new patient showed up one day in the office. His name was Ludwig Krüger—Professor Ludwig Krüger. Krüger was an older man—sixty-five years old—who was also German and was now living with his family in Panama City, a Gulf coast town along US 98, between Tallahassee and Pensacola, a little over a one-hour drive to Dr. Peltz's Panacea office. Krüger had heard of his compatriot's great reputation locally and wanted to switch his primary care to him as there were no satisfactory doctors at the time around Panama City.

Professor Krüger's first medical visit more than confirmed his confidence in Dr. Peltz. As there was no time during the scheduled appointments, they agreed to have lunch a week later at Angelo's Seafood Restaurant, a famous waterfront establishment.[7] There, the two men started to share stories of their better days in Germany and their student days at the University of Göttingen.

"I got my doctorate in mathematics probably at least ten years before you got your medical degree," Krüger said.

"You look much younger than that, Ludwig," Dr. Peltz remarked, smiling. "You must have led a chaste life. No alcohol, no cigarettes, no drugs, no affairs, unlike most of us Germans."

"That is true, Ernest."

"So how was university life for you, Ludwig? I myself got a rigorous but wonderful medical education in Göttingen."

"Ah, those were the years, my friend, when our country was at the pinnacle of learning in every area, the envy of the world," Krüger said.

"Absolutely," Dr. Peltz agreed.

"I studied under world-renowned scientists and mathematicians, like Felix Klein and David Hilbert," Krüger continued, "but then, as Hitler came to power, Jews like you were mostly banned from universities, graduate schools, medical schools, and law schools. Or at least a strict quota was enforced. So the exodus of intellectual giants and scientists from Germany eventually became inevitable."

"Tell me more about your background. Are you religious, Ludwig?" asked Dr. Peltz.

"I am. I am a devout Catholic, as is my family. We Catholics were not kindly looked on either. We left Germany before the war because of our disgust with the Nazi Party's intensifying persecution of Jews, the Roma population, homosexuals, and anyone else who didn't fit Hitler's perverted notion of the pure Aryan race."[8] And by 1939, when we fortunately left, even Catholic Poles in Nazi German-occupied Poland were being subjugated and suppressed by the Third Reich."[9]

"Did you and your family come directly to America?" Dr. Peltz asked.

"Well, we managed to get visas to settle in the United States. On arrival, we first lived in New York."

"Du *machst bestimmt Witze!!*" Dr. Peltz thundered, banging his fist on the table joyfully. "You must be kidding! I did the same. But how on earth did you find a job as a mathematician?"

"Not at all easily," replied Krüger. "I was able to get employment only sporadically in public schools in poor neighborhoods, teaching algebra, geometry, and the like. Moving to other cities wasn't much better. So the highest levels at which I could find work were in community colleges. Searching for a university professorship was utterly futile. So I retired frustrated, but at least I now had freedom. We moved to Panama City to take advantage of the imminent real estate boom that was predicted in Florida. And since then, I have been able to make quite a bit of money in building motels and condominiums."

Without breaching boundaries of their professional relationship as doctor and patient, Peltz and Krüger bonded over common interests, like politics, academics, European history, and books; they became good friends, regardless of their religious differences.

At the same time, Martha continued to go to Ku Klux Klan meetings occasionally, much to Dr. Peltz's chagrin. When she left the house for these meetings, she carried her white robe and white hood on her arm, rather than donning them at home.

"See, that's where ah can see my longtime friends. Catch up on gossip and all that," Martha tried to explain to the doctor. "Hoping not to run into Otis, but we're all masked, and ah hang around with only them women."

"But Martha," Dr. Peltz said, "help me understand what's the real purpose of the Klan these days. I know about their history, but what now?"

"Now that they hear about all that civil rights stuff, the ni***rs are getting all uppity. The're still just ni***rs, you know. They'll always be dumb fools. Most of 'em won't even know how to vote. But same *schools*? No *sir*, never. And intermarriage is a sin before the Lord."

Dr. Peltz was taken aback, but he couldn't be too critical, he thought to himself. After all, something like this was propagated in his own country not so long ago by Hitler's Nazis against the Jews.

One night in the late fall of 1961, Martha was awakened by the roar of trucks outside on the street. Hiding behind a curtain, she looked out from a window. She saw three truckloads full of Klansman, many of them wearing their white hoods, scurrying around the front lawn in the dark. They had already planted a big, wooden cross, and now they were lighting it.

"F**k," she said aloud.

This brought Dr. Peltz limping down the stairs in his gown and slippers as fast as he could.

"What's going on out there?" he shouted as he came to the window. By now, the wooden cross was supporting a roaring fire. Most of the men were running back to their trucks, which took off immediately, with some empty liquor bottles flying out of them and breaking on the sidewalk below.

"Sonabitch!" Martha said. "Otis was behind this. Ah jist know it. Him and his stupid drunk Klan buddies."

"How do you know? It's so dark outside," said Dr. Peltz.

"Oh ah *know*. He was one of the men without a hood on. And I would recognize that sonabitch anywhere and anytime. He was the only one who stayed behind for a couple of minutes, standing on the lawn and admiring that thar burning cross."

8

Settling In

Dr. Peltz was determined to stay active in social circles. For the Sunday after the Klan incident, he had invited to his brunch Nick's parents, Lili and Stephen Wolff, Rachel and David Moran, and a couple of other FSU faculty members he had previously met, including an economist and an art historian, along with their spouses. He also invited his mathematician friend and patient, Professor Ludwig Krüger and his wife, Gertrude, from Panama City.

"Dr. Peltz," David Moran said, turning to the doctor, "you have quite a collection of art on these walls. Is this a hobby of yours?"

"It's much more than a hobby," replied Dr. Peltz. "My passion for art began as a child and then emanated from my frequent visits to museums in Berlin and other cities in Germany before the war."

"Did all these nice paintings come from Germany?" Lili Wolff asked, as the others began to gather around the doctor.

"No," Dr. Peltz replied. "After I became settled in New York, I started to have the means to buy some authentic artwork. Not at auctions, mind you. I could never afford to bid for those masterpieces. I went to all the art dealers and fine art stores, not just in New York but all over the country and even in France looking for those undervalued or neglected gems. I hope you all enjoy them as you walk around … and please do help yourselves to the canapés and hors d'oeuvres, along with your drink," he said to his guests, who then dispersed to more closely examine each painting.

All the guests were instantly struck by the collection when they first entered. They strolled past an unfinished painting by Seurat using his familiar pointillism technique, a Toulouse-Lautrec, and lesser-known late nineteenth century European works. One that didn't stand out, so it didn't get as much attention from his guests, was a small pastel drawing of ballet dancers. It was sketched entirely in yellow, chamoisee, ochre, ecru, and other lighter shades of brown. But on this Sunday morning, the FSU art historian was the one who was entranced by it, gazing from different angles and distances with his chin perpetually propped up by a hand. He barely moved for quite a while.

"Yes, it's a Degas," Dr. Peltz said, startling the art historian as he slipped over to his side.

"I can't believe it. Do you have a magnifying glass by any chance, Dr. Peltz?"

"I certainly do." Peltz hurried off to his study to get one.

Others now began to gather around the small painting. After analyzing the sketch further, the art historian declared:

"I thought it was a forgery at first, but now I know it's the original. *This* is the long-lost *Five Dancing Women* by Edgar Degas, painted in midcareer! As you can see, it depicts these beautiful ballet dancers together in midperformance. It's perhaps the best example of the painter's many efforts to capture the most nuanced movements of the human body. It's absolutely remarkable. Extraordinary, in fact!"

"What do you mean by 'long-lost,' Ronald?" asked David Moran.

"Well, it was owned by Baron Mor Lipot Herzog, who had the largest private art collection in Hungary before the war—"

"Oh yes," David interrupted. "Now I remember hearing about that collection and what happened to it when I was in school in Budapest."

"When the baron died," continued the art history professor, "followed by his wife, the collection was passed down to their children, one of whom died in a Nazi labor camp. By late 1944, toward the end of World War II, the Nazi puppet government of Hungary allowed the German Nazis to seize precious artwork from the homes of wealthy Jews as those people were being rounded up for trains to concentration camps. The Herzog family tried to save their art by hiding the works in the cellar of one of their factories, but they were discovered and taken.[10] Today, many of the stolen art treasures have been recovered and are on display in museums all over the world. But this one was never found."

The art professor removed his glasses and gazed directly at Dr. Peltz.

"Dr. Peltz, where, may I ask, did you get this?"

"I bought it at one of those more inconspicuous art dealers in New York," he replied. "It was being stored along with junk, hidden and unmarked among a motley collection of less valuable paintings lying on the bare, dirty floor of the store's basement, can you believe it?"

"How much did it cost?" came a question from the group.

"Oh, I don't remember, maybe around $100."

"Thank you so much, Ronald, for educating us," said Dr. Peltz as he quickly turned to briskly walk away.

While this conversation was going on inside, Martha took Rachel Moran, that is *Dr.* Rachel Moran, out to the mansion's garden. The reputable landscaper and experienced gardener Dr. Peltz had hired to create his greenery along the sides of the house and in the back created a sight to behold. There were daffodils, dogwoods; tulips; irises; white, red, peach, and burgundy red oleander, beautiful but poisonous; and roses, as well as other flower plants native to the Deep South. They were a mixture of long-lived perennials, short-term annuals, and seasonal bulbs, all gloriously blooming at different times of the year in striking colors and with distinct fragrances. The different kinds of flowering plants were grouped together in clearly marked, separate flower beds; narrow gravel pathways allowed access to each grouping.

"After I moved in," Martha told Rachel, "there was no longer any need for a regular gardener because I had always loved flowers. I knew a lot about them, and so I became the caretaker of the gardens."

Rachel, who Martha still called *"Dr.* Moran," shared the same pastime with Martha and told her that. So the two of them strolled through the flower beds, identifying most of the flowers and talking about each type as they passed by, conversing as practically amateur botanists.

With time, Rachel and Martha became friends. Each was fascinated by the other's background. Rachel sensed that Martha was lonely for female friendship. So she invited Martha to come up to Tallahassee and have lunch with her at the historic Tallahassee Garden Club, located near downtown on North Calhoun Street.

When the time came, Rachel was waiting for her in the driveway. "Let me give you a quick tour," she offered, as a valet took Martha's car away to park it.

Inside the pre-Civil War house was a spacious, sun-filled

dining room with lace curtains over its tall windows. Classic Chiavari chairs were placed around tables of different sizes, all covered with white tablecloths and set with gleaming silverware.

The dining room was half-filled mostly with women tastefully dressed, many wearing colorful Sunday dress hats. Rachel kept looking at Martha, who appeared to be overcome by the elegance of the place. They sat down at a reserved table, facing each other. Rachel started the conversation by telling Martha her own difficult background in Europe, without going into detail. Martha said that she had never been outside the Florida panhandle, dropped out of school in the sixth grade, and by necessity grew up as a narrow-minded and inarticulate woman.

Two older women sitting nearby now leaned into each other whispering, covering their mouths with their hands, and every now and then glancing over to look at Martha. Rachel overheard one of the women saying, "White trash," but she was relieved to see that Martha didn't hear it.

Rachel, smiling easily and often, took a sincere interest in Martha, putting her guest at ease right away. When lunch was served in fine chinaware, Martha gasped.

"Oh mah god. Ah have never seen anythin' like this," she said rather loudly, turning some heads toward her.

"Well," Rachel said, "you'll be seeing more of it and more of the world from now on. I am sure of it, Martha."

With her elbows now on the table to lean in toward Martha, Rachel revealed something that was hidden under her long sleeve: around her wrist was an antique, solid silver bracelet with a gold trim.

"How beautiful!" Martha said, pointing to it with a soft gasp.

Rachel released the clasp and handed the bracelet to Martha.

"Why, look here, some engraving on the inside. Whut duz it say?"

Rachel took it back and squinted to try to read the engraving. "'Dr. Levi Ráhelm. ELTE. 1948,' I think. Yes, that's what it is," she said.

Rachel continued her story. "You know, Martha, my parents perished in a concentration camp somewhere in Europe during the World War—we Jewish people call it the Holocaust—and my closest living relative afterward was my aunt Anna. She gave me this bracelet when I graduated from medical school in Budapest in 1948. 'Levi' was my family name. 'Ráhelm' was my given name. It translates to 'Rachel.'" The 'ELTE' is the acronym of the medical school, 'Eötvös Loránd Tudományegyetem.' I remember Aunt Anna telling me the bracelet was an authentic Victorian piece."

Rachel and Martha then exchanged some more words about each other's backgrounds and interests, but both women clearly avoided uncomfortable conversations about the secrets and tragedies in their respective lives. At least for now. Hereafter, lunches at the Garden Club or at more informal diners downtown became a matter of course for them at Rachel's insistence, as her work permitted.

9

Metamorphosis

Over time, during conversations, Rachel discerned Martha's remarkable progress in her adult classes in Crawfordville. One of the teachers who happened to be Rachel's patient remarked to her that Martha's pure native intelligence was extraordinary and was being wasted. She also told Rachel that she and other teachers were pushing Martha into accelerated classes that now also included social sciences. In fact, Rachel found out that Martha successfully enrolled to audit a basic course in botany at FSU.

From the time they first met at Dr. Peltz's home, Rachel had recognized Martha's initially subdued gregariousness and amiability. At one of their lunches, Martha told Rachel that she was even making friends among the college students.

Martha had stopping calling Rachel "Dr. Moran." At that lunch, Martha was excited to tell Rachel that Dr. Peltz told her recently that he was pleased with her performance and efficiency in running his medical office and was now paying her to work full time there. He also said that his patients loved her.

Rachel also perceived a substantive change in Martha's confidence in speaking. Her vocabulary had greatly expanded, and she was beginning to be at some ease conversing in full sentences and articulating logical trains of thought. With the keen observational prowess of a physician, Rachel also recognized the subtilty of Martha gradually losing her southern accent when talking with new friends and colleagues. But much to her amusement, Rachel also saw Martha readily reverting to her southern drawl when she was with long-term acquaintances. When Rachel mentioned this to her on another occasion, Martha facetiously called herself "bilingual."

10

Symphony No. 2 in E Major

Dr. Peltz asked Martha to join him for a Saturday afternoon tea to which they were invited by Ilona Dohnányi, the recently widowed wife of Ernst von Dohnányi. Dohnányi was a world-renowned composer, conductor, and pianist who had spent the last decade of his prolific international career in Tallahassee, teaching at FSU's School of Music.[11] The Dohnányis had immigrated here from their native Hungary just as the Soviet-backed Communist regime was tightening its vise on all aspects of life there, including the arts. Martha didn't quite know what to expect but went along anyway.

They drove to Mrs. Dohnányi's lovely home in the upscale Tallahassee neighborhood of Waverly Hills. The quiet streets here were lined with stately live oak trees, their branches draped with Spanish moss to create a practically continuous canopy of shade over the road. The expansive, redbrick ranch house appeared to be only recently constructed, but its inside emanated the warm comfort of Old World wealth. Ilona opened the door and tried to shake hands with Dr. Peltz who, instead, lifted hers to kiss it. She had heard all about Dr. Peltz, whose reputation as a physician had spread fast and wide. However, this was the first time Ilona had seen him in person. Dr. Peltz introduced Martha, to whom Mrs. Dohnányi presumed he was married, but Dr. Peltz jumped in to explain their relationship. Ilona, though still in mourning, was a genuinely charming and exuberant hostess who instantly made Martha feel at home by hugging her. She ushered them into the spacious living room. Its centerpiece was the grand Steinway piano at which the maestro rehearsed and composed. The beautiful hardwood floor was partly covered by large, colorful Persian rugs.

Already there were Professor Stephen Wolff and his wife, Lili, along with their son, Nick, who sat on a cushion on the floor, Rachel and David Moran, and two other couples they didn't know, former faculty colleagues of Ernst at the School of Music along with their wives. Ilona made the introductions. A maid then brought in a silver tray with bone China plates, cups and saucers, silverware and napkins, along with freshly brewed pots of tea, placing them on a long tea station covered with a white tablecloth, which had been already placed against a wall. Then she came back from the kitchen with a tiered silver cake stand filled with finger sandwiches, cucumber and mint, smoke salmon and cream cheese, and eggs with watercress.

Ilona played the LP recording of the first movement of her husband's composition, *Symphony No. 2 in E Major*, conducted by himself with the BBC Philharmonic Orchestra. Martha had never heard anything like this, but by the end of the piece she was guardedly smiling. After reminiscences of Ernst von Dohnányi were exchanged by those who had known him, conversation turned to a variety of topics including the recent presidential election and the ongoing Cold War, which everyone took very seriously. Martha listened raptly and even interjected some thoughts about how difficult it must have been for all these special people in the room, all of European descent, to assimilate into life in the Deep South. Much to the surprise of Dr. Peltz, Martha even spoke decidedly in support of the civil rights movement that was well under way throughout the country, especially here, and how it was "about time."

Several people in the room were smoking cigarettes, even Martha when she was offered one. Rachel, who was a non-smoker, rubbed her irritated eyes every now and then. She kept curiously glancing at Dr. Peltz, even when he wasn't talking, apparently in deep thought. He didn't take notice.

The conversation shifted from Martha's mention of civil rights to issues related to the Holocaust and its aftermath, which was only fifteen years in the past. Most in the room were Jewish and were somehow profoundly affected by it. The Dohnányis weren't Jewish, but it was well known by then that the maestro was a proactive supporter of Jews, had resigned from all organizations worldwide that banned Jews from membership, and even used his personal fame to rescue Jewish musicians by arranging for them to leave Europe wherever they felt targeted for persecution.

As the topic was pursued, Rachel became suddenly and strangely detached, with unblinking eyes still fixated on Dr. Peltz, and remained silent. David, her husband, even turned to her and whispered, "Are you all right, Rachel? Is it the smoke?"

"I don't feel great," she replied softly, "but it'll be OK."

A few minutes later, Rachel silently stood up and walked over to Mrs. Dohnányi to ask where the bathroom was. She then stayed in the bathroom for quite a long time. When she came out, she looked ashen, distraught and perspiring. David walked right over to her while others looked up with concern.

"Do you want to go home, Rachel?" he asked in a low voice.

"I think we had better do that. I don't know what's come over me. I really feel dizzy and wobbly. Like being seasick."

David turned to Mrs. Dohnányi and begged her pardon for needing to leave early. Ilona knew something was wrong and promptly went over to hold Rachel's shoulders.

"Of course, my dear," she said looking into her now vacant eyes and smiling, eyes that now appeared sunken. "I do hope you feel better soon. It was such a pleasure to have you here today. We'll do it another time."

"Yes, yes," David and Rachel replied simultaneously. "Thank you so much for your gracious hospitality."

By now, almost everyone in the room was helplessly looking at Rachel. The couple waved to others and the men stood up as David, supporting Rachel, walked out the door.

11

A Stranger at the Door

On a fall midday, when Dr. Peltz was away doing his research in New York, the doorbell rang at his Apalachicola house. Only Martha was at home, and she opened the door. A pale, stocky woman with a wrinkled face and hooded eyes, wearing no makeup, stood at the doorway. She was dressed in black.

"My name is Hannah Spielman. I was Ernst Peltz's former wife. You must be Martha," she said stepping inside.

"He has told me about you," a shocked Martha said, placing her hand to her open mouth, with her eyes also wide open. "But he said you had … died … from a stroke."

"I am not surprised," the visitor replied. "That's what he tells everybody. May I come in?"

"Of course, of course," Martha stumbled, leading her to the living room and pointing to a comfortable armchair for her to sit in.

"Can I offer you anything?"

"Just a glass of water. It's been a long journey."

As Martha handed it to her, the woman blurted out. "Are you married to him?"

"No, and—" Martha couldn't finish.

"Do you have sexual relations with him?"

"Never," Martha replied, taken aback by the forwardness of the woman.

"Well, then what are you doing living here?"

Martha was speechless and thought about escorting this impertinent woman out the front door. It even crossed her mind that she was a fraud, not at all the doctor's wife as she claimed to be. But Martha's curiosity got the better of her.

"He hired me as his live-in housekeeper. We sleep in different parts of the house," Martha said.

"All right, all right, Martha," Hannah Spielman said, but not without being able to mask the subtlest mischievous smile of disbelief that now appeared on her face.

"So now tell me why you are here and how you found Dr. Peltz. He is not here now, you know?" Martha said, visibly annoyed.

"I knew he wasn't going to be here and that's why I came now. I am here to help you, not him. I caught sight of him last night in an Upper East Side German restaurant, sitting at a back booth with his old friends, all of them laughing heartily, smoking like chimneys, and drinking beer from big steins. I left immediately, unseen. As soon as I saw that he was in New York, I booked an early-morning ticket on Eastern Airlines to come to Tallahassee through Atlanta. Then I rented a Hertz car, and here I am!"

"And how did you know where he was living?" Martha asked again.

"That was easy. The gynecologist I work for in New York is a member of the American Medical Association. She just called the AMA office in Chicago for me and found out that

Dr. Ernest Peltz lives in Apalachicola, Florida. A familiar place. We used to come to this area of the Florida panhandle for vacation when we were married."

"And what about me? How did you find out about me?" Rachel asked.

"That was easy too. I called the Apalachicola city hall and got the address of this house. I also asked if anyone else was legally living in this house, and they told me there was a Martha Langston."

"So how on earth are you trying to f***ing help me?" Martha asked, relapsing to her use of profanity, angry at this woman for her shameless intrusion.

"I thought I should tell you some things about Ernest's background you may not know. He is a very private man, as you have surely found out, so he doesn't like to talk to anyone about his past," said Hannah.

"Do you know things about him we don't know here?" Martha asked.

"Possibly," replied Hannah. "It took me years of a struggling marriage to extract bits and pieces of information from him about his background and to try to piece it all together."

"Are you going to tell me everything is a lie? You know everyone here loves the man; all his patients are devoted to him, and he's made lots of friends in Tallahassee within the medical community and with the Jewish people."

"No, I don't think everything is a lie. But he is a secretive man," Hannah explained. "You know, in our Brooklyn apartment Ernest kept his small study that was locked at all times. One of the unbreakable rules he listed for me in writing after I moved in to live with him was to never ever set foot in that room, not even to clean it, which he insisted on doing himself. And I was never to allow anyone else to enter that room."

"Now that you mention it," Martha said, "that's exactly what he has done here. His study is sacred, he told me."

"Toward the end of our marriage, when our differences had become irreconcilable," Hanna continued, "I hired a locksmith to pick the lock to his study while he was at work."

"So what did you find?" Martha asked, leaning forward in her chair with attentive interest.

"Most of the stuff in his files was in German, which I couldn't translate, except for a few words here and there that resembled Yiddish. But one file contained English language documents concerning his immigration to America. There were letters to him from the US Immigration and Naturalization Service, dated around 1949 and 1950. They had the seal of the Department of Justice on their letterhead. They all referred to Ernest being granted a visa under the sponsorship of the CIA," said Hannah.

"CIA?" asked Martha.

"Central Intelligence Agency. The government's main agency that pursues intelligence to ensure national security. They have a big workforce of people all over the world to secretly search for threats to the United States."

"So," Martha was momentarily confused, "... so are you saying that Dr. Peltz did not come to this country *before* the outbreak of the war to escape the Nazi ... persecution of Jews?" She was now bewildered.

"It's called anti-Semitism, my dear. Is that what he told you?" Hannah asked. "No, he didn't leave Germany to escape anti-Semitism. He stayed there through the war and for several years after it."

Martha frowned. "So he lied to me. He lied to everyone in this community. Is he even Jewish, like he tells everyone?'"

"I don't have any reason to think that he lied about that," Hannah responded. "He just told me that he wasn't a very observant Jew. He said he couldn't be that because he was so busy with his job all the time."

"So he came to this country about 1950?"

"Yes, that's what he told me."

"Well, so what's all this stuff about the CIA that you mentioned?"

Hannah Spielman then described to Martha what she knew. She explained that right after World War II ended, there was a fierce competition between the United States and the Soviet Union—Russia—to recruit as quickly as possible many of the top Nazi scientists, doctors, and university professors who had evaded trial for being war criminals. The government wanted them to work here to support our country's growing intelligence operations that were now aimed at the Soviet Union. And the Russians did likewise against us, as we entered the Cold War. We know that thousands of Nazis were covertly, secretively granted entry into the United States around that time, between about 1948 and 1952 through the CIA and other federal intelligence agencies.[12] Even the president of the United States didn't know about this covert operation.

"Oh my God," Martha interrupted. "So Dr. Peltz was a *Nazi*?"

"No, no," replied Hannah with a quick smile. "I never heard anything about that. Remember, Ernest *is* Jewish after all."

Hannah went on to tell Martha that Dr. Peltz was not only an excellent doctor, but he also did some medical research in Germany. Dr. Peltz had told Hannah that that his research concerned the human brain. His goal was to discover what was different in the brains of mentally ill people compared to those who are sane. When our spies and CIA operatives found Dr. Peltz after the war and learned about his medical background, they promptly recruited him to live in America to help in the country's Cold War efforts.

"What did they want him to do?" Martha said.

In fact Dr. Peltz was assigned to work under a man named Dr. Harold Abramson, who had an office and a small laboratory in the General Laboratory Building of Mount Sinai Hospital in Manhattan, with a medical faculty appointment at Columbia. He also had a private practice office at 135 East Fifty-Eighth Street. Abramson's research was generously funded by the CIA, with the money being funneled through the Josiah Macy Foundation, which served as a front to separate the CIA from being his direct source of financial support. Abramson's and his then assistant Dr. Peltz's research concerned alterations of the mind and mechanisms of mind control. This was a peculiar arena of research for Dr. Harold Abramson because he was a clinical allergist by certification and had never had any training in psychiatry or neurology. Their mind control research came under the code names of "Project Bluebird," "Project Artichoke, and "Project Paperclip," parts of a top secret MKUltra operation sponsored covertly by the CIA.[13] Mount Sinai was far from the only institution where these CIA-funded experiments were being conducted. Many other locations in the United States were engaged, including prestigious universities like Columbia, Emory, Harvard, and the Universities of California (Berkeley), Illinois, and Wisconsin.[14]

Dr. Peltz met Hannah at Mount Sinai Hospital where she worked as a technician for another, unrelated physician, an obstetrician-gynecologist named Gisella Perl, whose office was in the same building, a few floors above Dr. Abramson's. Gisella Perl was one of the most notable, heroic survivors of Auschwitz, where she saved the lives of innumerable Jewish women.[15]

From the time they met and throughout their marriage, Dr. Peltz refused to give Hannah any information, much less details, of what he was doing with Dr. Abramson, repeatedly asserting that it was "top secret." In fact, Abramson was doing clinical research using human experimentation with subjects who had not given consent, observing and recording the effects of various mind-altering, illicit drugs and plant derivatives, ultimately designed to be used as weapons in the Cold War. Being at best a sham psychiatrist, Abramson's "experiments" were completely nonscientific in structure.

On one occasion, while Dr. Peltz was working under him, Abramson became intimately involved in a tragically misconceived experiment conducted by CIA officials on unwitting colleagues whose afterdinner cocktails were spiked with LSD at a retreat to which they were invited at Deep Creek Lake[16] in western Maryland. One of the men, Frank Olson, didn't recover from the hallucinogenic effects of LSD and shortly thereafter, while staying in New York overnight at the Statler Hotel[17] before his scheduled psychiatric appointment with Dr. Abramson the next day, in the middle of the night, he crashed through the window of his room, number 1018a, on the tenth floor of the hotel, right onto the Seventh Avenue sidewalk below, instantly killing him. Officially, he committed suicide, but foul play hasn't been ruled out to this day.[18]

"After that," Hannah Spielman continued, now having Martha's rapt attention, "our marriage disintegrated. He was spending all his days at work and most of his nights at some kind of secret men's club for World War II veterans, who met at different places every time to ensure their privacy. His secretiveness about everything, not just his work, approached paranoid levels, I thought. We essentially stopped communicating altogether, and one day he just matter-of-factly told me to leave. He wanted a divorce because he said he wanted to live alone."

"Mah God, are there any other bad things ah need tuh know about Dr. Peltz?" Martha asked, then continued. "You know, in the beginning Dr. Peltz was so good to me. He even urged me to take those adult education classes to start a career and be independent. But now, recently, he has become more abrupt with me, like angry sometimes. And he has become much more reclusive, just like you said."

Hannah stood up and handed Martha a piece of paper.

"I have taken much of your time, but I felt compelled to inform you of what I have learned about the man. I've had suspicions about other things concerning Ernest, but I don't want to talk about them because I have no evidence to support those concerns. You and I are from very different backgrounds in every way. But I do know now that you are a good woman, Martha, and I will help you any way I can in the future to ensure that you have a good life. There, she said, pointing to the paper she had just given to Martha, "that's my home phone number, my number at work, and my address."

"You are so generous," Martha said as she escorted Hannah to the door.

12

The Colored Only Office

Martha's life became more demanding as she settled into her new position as the receptionist for Dr. Peltz's Colored Only office. At first, when Dr. Peltz informed her of this, she was taken aback by the thought of having been demoted. She sulked for a while, resentful of Dr. Peltz's order.

Trailer trash, that's all you are, Martha thought after settling into her desk chair as the clinic opened. *I am stuck here, doing this.* She recognized that she had been castigating herself for not being better ever since Dr. Peltz reassigned her to the other clinic. For days and nights, she fixated on her damned inadequacy now that she had seen what it was like to leave the trailer park.

Yet, at the same time, Martha's mind was imperceptibly transforming into a more open view of society and culture.

She suddenly snapped out of her self-pity and remembered the days Rachel and her friends remarked on how speedily she had cruised through every course available in her adult education program.

Resurrecting her self-esteem, it dawned on Martha how

her world view of prejudice or tolerance, exclusiveness or inclusiveness, hatred or at least acceptance, was undergoing a subconscious metamorphosis. Others had recognized and talked to her about her sheer intelligence and ambition. But she just waved them off. Now, finally, her drive and ambitiousness fully unleashed, she was able to pass the General Education Development (GED) test for high school equivalency in record time, and she was already thinking about enrolling at FSU part time. So her hurt feelings about being assigned to the Colored Only clinic quickly changed to viewing it as a propitious challenge.

Initially, Martha found her new job and interactions with only Black people admittedly distasteful and noxious, but this quickly dissipated. She now also had to deal with the various barriers these impoverished people encountered getting access to even minimal health care. They were either unemployed or engaged mostly as domestic workers or farmhands, the two occupations that were explicitly excluded from the Social Security program that had been enacted in 1935 as part of the New Deal. The types of insurance coverage provided by Social Security programs were only slowly broadened beginning in 1950, remaining mostly ineffective for these disadvantaged patients[19] as there were no local agencies available to help them navigate the system.

So much of this burden fell on Martha, on top of all the scheduling and accounting she had to do in the office. In the absence of telephones in the homes of most patients, she would have to drive to their houses after office hours to tell them about their upcoming appointments. For some patients, the racially imposed bureaucratic obstacles were too complex, perhaps intentionally, and required Dr. Peltz's intervention. But Dr. Peltz made it clear to Martha that he didn't want to hear about them. They weren't his job, he kept saying to her.

He became increasingly annoyed and demanding when she approached him with such questions. If she reached a dead end in pursuing payment on behalf of a patient, Dr. Peltz would turn red in the face and abruptly tell her to "figure it out yourself."

Another job Martha assumed in this clinic, which she didn't have to do in the other one, was maintenance of the small "free" pharmacy Dr. Peltz had created. Despite his recent treatment of her, Martha was sincerely moved by Dr. Peltz's altruism toward these impoverished people.

Managing inventory, reordering drugs in a timely manner as they were running out, and writing progress notes for each patient receiving these medications as to their mood and behavior had become quite demanding. Dr. Peltz had ordered her to keep *precise* records of which patients used which medications, in what doses, and when. To Martha's relief, Dr. Peltz insisted on dispensing the medications himself.

Dr. Peltz was particularly obsessive about the accuracy of the medication records. He was painstakingly meticulous with correcting Martha's short narratives and pointing out her smallest mistakes.

"Look here. Mr. Robinson's dose was *not* 50 mg daily," Dr. Peltz yelled at her, pointing to the mistake. "It's 50 mg *twice* a day! Don't you understand what a catastrophic mistake it would have been if I hadn't caught it?" As Martha tried to respond, he belted out in his native language, "Bist du völlig blind? Wo ist dein Kopf?" His fit of rage now made him look and sound like a mad man, shaking, spitting as he bellowed, with veins becoming visible in his neck, and his face turning deep red.

After he collected himself, Dr. Peltz asked Martha to sit down across from him. "After all," he said quietly and hoarsely, "I have been giving those *verdammt* drugs away free of charge, don't you know? I have a responsibility to review the records every day and, if necessary, reprimand you any time I find even the smallest of errors."

Fortunately, ordering, receiving, and shelving the medications became quite easy because they were all being sent from the same pharmacy in Maryland, directly to Dr. Peltz.

As patients and their family members returned for follow-up appointments, Martha began to take a genuine interest in their lives and problems. Only a few were reluctant to converse, usually because they were still suspicious of dealing with White health-care professionals.[20] Most of the others got to like Martha, and she, in turn, took a liking to them.

13

The CIA

Later in the week, Martha confessed to Rachel how almost viscerally repulsed she was by the patients there when she first started in the Colored Only clinic. Martha told Rachel how she wrestled with herself in bed sleeplessly for the past two nights, feeling so ashamed of herself for her noxious and instinctive reaction to being reassigned to the Colored Only clinic. Rachel already knew about Martha's racist views and even her membership in the women's auxiliary of the Ku Klux Klan.[21] Rachel didn't appear to be at all startled by this.

"Don't ruminate about those thoughts, Martha. You lost that baggage a few years ago," Rachel said.

Martha then told Rachel about the strange visit from Dr. Peltz's former wife.

"She just rang the doorbell, and thar she stood when I opened the door. Hanna Spielman," started Martha.

"Wow. But I thought you told me his wife had died," said Rachel.

"Well, that's what Dr. Peltz told me. A stroke, he said, but thar she was in flesh and blood."

"Are you sure it was her?" Rachel asked.

"That crossed my mind also, but it really was her, not a ghost. On the doorstep, unannounced," replied Martha. "She said she wanted to meet me to talk with me about Dr. Peltz at a time when the woman knew he would be away from Apalachicola."

"Was he away?"

"Yes."

"And how did she know where the doctor was living or who you were?" Rachel persisted in disbelief.

"Oh, she told me she had done a lot of searchin' about all those things, Rachel."

"So do tell, Martha, what did she say about Dr. Peltz?"

"Well, first of all he didn't escape from the Nazis before World War II broke out, as he had been telling everybody in this area. He *is* Jewish, she said, but he stayed in Germany after the war until he got a visa to work in the States in 1952. He got the visa to do some kind of medical research project at a hospital in New York, but Mrs. Spielman could never get him to talk about it," continued Martha.

"Which hospital?"

"I can't remember. Mount something."

"Mount Sinai?"

"That's it," Martha snapped back.

"And did she say who paid for his position at Mount Sinai Hospital?"

"Some kinda Foundation, ..." Martha hesitated, probing her memory. "I can't remember the name," she said. Something like Macy, I think. But she did say the money came originally from the CIA."

14

Martha Moves

Given all that she had recently learned about Dr. Peltz and her increasingly frosty relationship with him, Martha had been for some time contemplating moving out. She found a very modest, small house for sale for $30,000 just outside Panacea. She had saved enough money to mortgage it now at $10,000.

Martha confronted Dr. Peltz at home about her decision and reassured him that she would continue to serve as his housekeeper and as receptionist at the Colored Only clinic. Dr. Peltz's response was apathetic; he shrugged his shoulders.

So Martha made the move. She asked Hunter to help out, repairing the interior and doing the painting in her new house. She paid him for it. Martha herself scrubbed the bathroom and the tiny kitchen. Dr. Peltz let her keep the car and clothes she had purchased, for which she expressed much gratitude. But Dr. Peltz said that he no longer needed her as his housekeeper. In fact, he made it clear that he didn't want to *see* her there anymore and asked her to give him back the keys to the house. He would continue to pay her salary for the receptionist job.

The next time Martha had lunch in Tallahassee with Rachel, for whom she had finally summoned the courage to call by her first name, Rachel had some disturbing news to tell her.

"Something is going on—I'm not sure exactly what—with Dr. Peltz," Rachel started. "Word is spreading among a few of my physician colleagues that Dr. Peltz has been holding a young woman in his house against her will. I presume they are referring to you, Martha. They also say the young woman is his sex slave and that the Jewish doctor is having wild, drug-fueled orgies on Sunday afternoons, sacrilegiously after everyone else has been to church—"

"That's crazy," Martha interrupted. "He invites friends on Sunday afternoons for brunch. You know that, Rachel; you've been there. It's a chance to sit around to discuss world affairs and other things of interest. And then, as you know, some go fishing in Dr. Peltz's new boat. That's it."

"I know that, Martha, but these rumors are going to damage his reputation. I've even heard that they talk to each other about Dr. Peltz being the mastermind of a Jewish conspiracy all across the South to destroy the cherished culture and way of life of White Christians."

"That's bull****!" said Martha, angrily. "I know we are beginning to hear about different sides of Dr. Peltz, but I've been living in the same house with him for quite a while, and I would surely know about all those things. As much as I've come to dislike him, Dr. Peltz would never be capable of hurting a single soul."

"How can you be certain that everything Mrs … what's her name … yes, Spielman told you was true?" Rachel asked skeptically.

"I can't be sure," Martha responded, "but she sure sounded sincere and level-headed. Which reminds me, I did call her in Brooklyn after the visit. She said the name of the physician Dr. Peltz worked for at Mount Sinai was Harold Abramson."[22]

Rachel wrote it down. "Anything else about him?"

"Only that he was an allergist."[22]

"That's odd," Rachel said. "Why would an allergist be doing research for the CIA?"

After a pause, Rachel continued, "But let's talk about more pleasant things, Martha, like how is your new house?"

15

The Krügers in Panama City

Almost everyone in this region of Florida probably knew of his remarkable professional reputation, affability, and gregarious personality. Dr. Peltz felt more and more welcome knowing that he was earning the goodwill of his growing network of acquaintances. And yet he rued over the fact that he didn't have any real friends in this community. In particular, he missed the company of German compatriots who were intellectual peers. With his house now almost empty, he became keenly aware, perhaps for the first time in his life, of a strange sense of loneliness creeping in. So when he received a gracious letter from Professor Krüger's wife, Gertrude, inviting him to come for a weekend lunch at their home in Panama City, that pleasant and unexpected surprise brightened his day.

On a Sunday morning, Dr. Peltz drove down to Panama City, bringing with him a box of chocolates for Gertrude, a time-honored European custom. He was just hoping they wouldn't melt on the way.

The Krügers' house was easy to find, across the street

from the pristine, sparkling white-sand beach. It was a modest, low-slung but sprawling ranch-style house with a red-brick exterior, attached to a one-car garage. There was a small front yard of only grass. Next door was a Waffle House. For a fleeting moment, Dr. Peltz became self-conscious about his own mansion, where he now lived alone.

He was warmly greeted at the door by Professor Krüger and Gertrude and ushered in from the bright sun into the dark interior. Stepping inside, he sensed a musty, dank odor and heard the loudly rattling and gurgling sound of fans in the window air conditioners. He quickly accommodated.

The Krügers' oldest son, Herbert, was already there, having coffee at the kitchen table. Bert, as he was called, was a tall and handsome young man. He stood up, ramrod straight, to shake Dr. Peltz's hand with a firm grip. He did everything but salute.

Professor Krüger came over with a proud smile on his face.

"Bert was just promoted to lieutenant from lieutenant junior grade in the US Coast Guard, you know, " he said.

"What an honor," Dr. Peltz responded, "and you are so young!"

"Not young, sir. I am thirty," Bert proclaimed.

After they sat down for brunch in the modest dining room, Dr. Peltz started asking Bert what exactly he does as a coast guard officer. Peltz admitted that he didn't know anything about the coast guard. For a flash, Peltz couldn't help thinking that it was like the *Kriegsmarine* of the Nazi Wehrmacht.[23]

"I am stationed here in Panama City," Bert began, "and our area of responsibility extends more than fifty miles offshore in the Gulf and stretches over almost two hundred miles of coastline—"

"And you are the *lieutenant* of it, my son!" interrupted Gertrude, standing up to hug Bert.

"Our job is to enforce maritime laws," Bert continued after catching his breath from the bear hug. "We do things like environmental protection, catching illegal activities like drug smuggling, ensuring the safety of people who sail far out into the Gulf, and being first responders for search and rescue operations. Especially our fishermen."

"Are there a lot of fishermen here?" asked Dr. Peltz.

"Oh yes, big time!" exclaimed Bert. "Panama City is well known for it. The fishing industry here essentially supports our local economy. Fresh seafood harvesting is the occupation of a large segment of the town's population. And, of course, as you might expect from the grueling work they do, major accidents can happen, like onboard injuries, falling overboard, and even drowning as they trawl with large, heavy nets."

Dr. Peltz had no idea about this and listened intently.

"Let me take you over to the station so that you can see what we do, although you are not permitted to enter certain high-security places."

"OK," Dr. Peltz said in a tentative voice.

"I have to get dressed. I keep a uniform here," said Bert.

He quickly returned in his well-pressed service dress blue uniform with two golden stripes on his jacket sleeves.

"Are you coming, Dad and Mom?"

"Naah! We have been there many times," said Gertrude. "You and Dr. Peltz just go on along … and Bert, show him the fishing boats."

The drive was short, about fifteen minutes, because the station was located inland from the beach, close to the Hathaway Bridge that crosses the bay into Panama City itself.

As they entered the grounds, there was tight security. Those at the gate promptly saluted Bert at attention, but Dr.

Peltz was ushered into a hut where he had to provide personal information and received a visitor permit for the day. The offices, meeting rooms, and cafeteria inside were brightly colored to offset the absence of windows, and they were immaculately clean. Bert showed his guest around and introduced him to some of the officers, telling them all that Dr. Peltz was a distinguished physician, internationally known, and by far the best in the Florida panhandle. This grandiloquent presentation, emphatically spoken by the newly promoted lieutenant, caused a few of the men to subconsciously make an ever-so-slight bow as they shook Peltz's hand.

After they left the grounds, Bert took Dr. Peltz to the various marinas, piers, slips, and docks from which the commercial fishermen worked, day and night. They were within easy walking distance of each other and to the coast guard station. But unlike the latter, the atmosphere here was chaotic and loud, reeking of freshly caught fish of all kinds. But Bert felt very much at home here as he knew many of the fishermen and greeted them by name.

Finally, Bert drove Dr. Peltz back to his parents' house, where his car was parked, but before parting Bert said:

"It has been a real pleasure to meet you, sir. My father has spoken so highly of you and now I can see why. I know you have a motorboat—"

"I don't use it myself, but my friends do," Dr. Peltz interrupted.

"Well, in any case," Bert said, fishing through his pockets to give Dr. Peltz a card, "if ever your boat gets into trouble for whatever reason, or one of your guests falls out of it," he continued chuckling with his hand to his mouth, "or if I can help you in any way, please don't hesitate to call me here at either of those number on my new business card. The top is my office numbers at the station and the bottom is my home number."

16

Bert's Pneumonia

Not more than a month after his visit with the Krügers in Panama City, Dr. Peltz got a frantic phone call at his office from Professor Krüger.

"Bert is really sick," Professor Krüger said. He is hospitalized at Tallahassee Memorial Hospital with some kind of pneumonia. He has been there for four days now, under the care of Dr. Calhoun—*Houston* Calhoun, I think is his first name—and he is getting worse every day. I talked to Dr. Calhoun today, and he says they are trying different antibiotics on him, but none of them seem to be working. Can you help in any way?"

"Let me see what I can do," replied Dr. Peltz in a tone intended to calm his friend and patient. "There are only two more patients on my schedule today, so after that, I'll drive to TMH as quickly as possible."

Dr. Peltz got Bert's room and phone numbers and called Bert to tell him he would be there shortly. Then, with considerable trepidation, he called Dr. Calhoun. Dr. Houston Calhoun was the chief of medicine.

Dr. Calhoun was well known and respected by the medical community. But on a previous occasion, after a medical staff meeting, he had pulled Dr. Peltz aside for a talk. At first Dr. Calhoun welcomed Dr. Peltz. But then he began to berate him for "stealing" patients away from his own practice as well as the patients of other physicians. Dr. Peltz responded that he had no idea where his new patients came from, they just came, and he was most certainly not stealing them. Dr. Calhoun then lectured him that as a German Jew, he was an alien, a greenhorn in this town, and he had better learn the customs and civility of the medical society hereabouts and to stop being uppity. Dr. Peltz was taken aback and just calmly asked Dr. Calhoun what he should do with a new patient—order them to go back to their previous physician?

"I understand your suspicion about when you thought I was redirecting your patients and those of other colleagues of yours to my practice. That was never the case, please believe me. Those patients *chose* me on their own—or maybe by recommendations from others—to be their doctor. I never said a single word of encouragement to any of them to take them from your practice. In fact, it wasn't until their first visits with me that I even knew they existed."

"Yes, yes, so come on now," the unappeased Dr. Calhoun said impatiently, "I don't have any time to waste. I don't need to know that Herbert Krüger is your patient's son. What do you want?"

"His father asked me to see him in the hospital strictly as a consultant only. You would remain in complete charge of his inpatient care, of course."

"You know, Peltz, this is ridiculous," snapped Dr. Calhoun. "He has already been seen by expert specialists in infectious and pulmonary diseases, and appropriate antibiotics were promptly started. So I don't know what the hell you expect to contribute to his management."

"But his diagnosis is not clear," replied Dr. Peltz, "and I was told he was not responding to those antibiotics."

"You just don't understand, do you?" Dr. Calhoun fired back. "He's got pneumonia. I don't know what's not clear to you. Pneumonia is pneumonia. He is getting the best treatment for it."

"But he shouldn't have pneumonia. He is a young, healthy man, and—"

"Damn it, man. I can't stop you from consulting on a patient when a next-of-kin formally requests it. Just do it, but don't expect us to follow your old-fashioned German recommendations; that's something we don't have to do here."

With that, Dr. Calhoun hung up. "What a disrespectful idiot that man is. And doesn't he realize how renowned I am? I am a credit to his damned hospital," he mumbled to himself, pacing up and down. "Who does he think he is? Probably one of those barely educated, xenophobic, and anti-Semitic 'old boy' southerners."

When Dr. Peltz arrived at Bert's bedside, he was in obvious respiratory distress, wearing an oxygen mask over his nose and mouth. He was awake and alert but strangely didn't recognize Dr. Peltz. Dr. Peltz asked him about other symptoms. Bert said he was coughing badly and had a terrible headache, but the nurses gave him only aspirin. Dr. Peltz had to raise his voice because it looked like Bert had some kind of a hearing loss. Dr. Peltz then completed a full physical examination. It was so thorough that he even took out an otoscope from his black doctor's bag to look inside Bert's ears. Not surprised, he saw some blood on the left ear's tympanic membrane.

"Aha!" he said to himself in a self-congratulatory tone as he stood up. Bert's lung exam was essentially normal, but his chest X-ray, which Dr. Peltz had looked at in the Radiology Department before coming up to the ward, showed extensive, fine markings in both lungs.

Dr. Peltz looked up the names of Bert's infectious diseases and pulmonary consultants in his chart at the nurses' station. He then called each of them, explaining who he was and why he was participating in Bert's care. Then, with an ever-so-slight tinge of presumptuousness, he said he thought he knew the diagnosis and why he was not responding to various antibiotics like penicillin, vancomycin, polymyxin, and cephalosporin.

The reception from these two doctors was gratifyingly different from Houston Calhoun's dismissiveness. In fact, since it was dinnertime, they both agreed to meet Dr. Peltz together in the hospital cafeteria.

The choices of watery shepherd's pie, undercooked chicken, a dish that vaguely resembled a fish, tasteless boiled carrot slices and asparagus, combined with that overpowering institutional cafeteria smell, a diabolical mix of bleach, mop water after cleaning up a big milk spill, hot dishwater, and fried grease, wasn't exactly appetizing, ... but Dr. Peltz's mission here was a much higher priority.

"I think he has a severe and complicated case of PPLO,[24] also known as the Eaton agent," Dr. Peltz began. "Complicated because I think he may also have meningitis and encephalitis caused by the same microorganism, as rare as it is."

"Why do you say that?" the pulmonologist asked.

"On my exam he had a stiff neck, nuchal rigidity with meningeal characteristics, and he didn't recognize me even though I met him at his parents' home just one month ago. There were no focal neurologic signs, but he clearly had an altered mental status," replied Dr. Peltz.

"And why do you say he has PPLO?"

"Textbook atypical pneumonia," Dr. Peltz noted. "Essentially clear lungs by auscultation but widely distributed, bilateral interstitial markings on X-ray."

"Anything else?"

"Oh yes, I almost forgot," Dr. Peltz said. "He has hemorrhagic myringitis. He had blood covering his eardrum on my otoscopic exam. Again, unusual but almost diagnostic of PPLO."

"What the *hell*," exclaimed the impressed infectious diseases specialist as the two doctors looked at each other, eyebrows raised in amazement of Dr. Peltz's knowledge and diagnostic skill.

"If anything, the patient appears to be deteriorating on his empiric antibiotics, so the question is why?" Dr. Peltz continued.

"Well, it could be—" the pulmonary specialist began to say before Dr. Peltz interrupted him.

"Well, scientists have begun to rename the PPLO microbe *Mycoplasma*. And a paper in the current issue of the journal *Nature* has reported for the first time actually visualizing the microbe under the microscope without the use of routine stains."

"Dr. Peltz, do you really read *Nature*? It's a purely scientific publication, way beyond the understanding of most physicians."

"Certainly," Dr. Peltz replied. "But it's only for my enjoyment. In this case, Bert Krüger needs a bronchoscopy. I would very much like to get a small sample of his bronchial epithelium. I have quite a lot of experience with microscopy, so I might be able to actually see the little bugs and make a firm diagnosis."

"Would it make any difference in treating him for … what

did you call it ... mycoplasma infection?" asked the infectious diseases specialist.

"It would indeed," Dr. Peltz replied. "The antibiotics he has been getting up to now all work to kill bacteria that have cell walls on their outside surfaces, targeting and destroying them. So using those antibiotics could not affect mycoplasma in the same way because they don't *have* a cell wall to attack," Dr. Peltz argued.

"Yes! How simple," exclaimed the infectious diseases consultant.

"So if we gave him antibiotics that can kill microorganisms that don't have a cell wall like mycoplasma, they may be effective," Dr. Peltz proposed.

"Like which ones? It seems we have used almost every one of them."

"Azithromycin and erythromycin come to mind," said Dr. Peltz. "I understand that a drug called doxycycline is in development, which should also be effective in the future."

When they stood to shake hands, the two hospital consultants expressed their awe of Dr. Peltz's intellect.

"Not so fast," Dr. Peltz warned. "I may not be right, you know."

Dr. Peltz wrote his opinion on Bert's medical chart. When Dr. Calhoun read it the next day, he was fuming. He went directly to the two consultants to ask their opinions and was taken aback when they both endorsed Dr. Peltz's opinion.

Two days after starting azithromycin, Bert's condition appeared to turn the corner. He no longer needed oxygen. And two days later all his symptoms had been resolved. He was picked up in the hospital lobby to go home with his parents and new fiancée.

17

Nick and Jimmy

By this time many of Dr. Peltz's contacts had found out that he left Germany after the war, in 1950, not in 1938 as he previously claimed.

Nick Wolff overheard his parents a couple of times talking in a lowered voice about Dr. Peltz. Before Nick was born, both of his parents had been apprehended by the Nazis during the war; his mother was assigned to Auschwitz, where she miraculously survived, unlike her brother who was killed in the gas chambers there. His father had also been taken away, in his case to a work camp in Ukraine, which might as well have been called a death camp. Having been persecuted and stripped of their citizenships and livelihoods for a full decade, Nazi Germans and their collaborators orchestrated the "Final Solution," which was the mass, assembly-line kind of slaughter and extermination of what ended up to be six million Jews, including women and children.

"Lili, I just don't have a good feeling about the good Dr. Peltz. The few times I have talked to him in Panacea or at the synagogue, he seemed so ... so secretive, so laconic," Nick's father, Stephen, said to his wife as Nick walked by them one evening. "As you have heard me say before, I am suspicious of Germans—or Hungarians for that matter—who left their country *after* the war was over and Communist regimes were taking power. Especially a Jew. What was a Jewish man doing in Germany during the war, and then why and how did he come to this country just a few years later?"

Nick sat down with his parents this time.

"You know my friend Jimmy Langston's mother, Martha?" Nick started, "well, she has left Dr. Peltz's house. They weren't getting along, I guess. Jimmy told me that Dr. Peltz's former wife came to visit Martha from New York to tell her more about him. She told her he had a locked study there, just like he has here, and Mrs. Peltz hired a locksmith to pick the lock of the New York study and found in it—"

Nick was breathless, talking fast and now taking a gulp. He continued even faster, "and found in it a whole bunch of letters organized in labeled files, really neat, almost all of them in German, so she couldn't understand them, and of course couldn't take them away to be translated so—"

"Those files would have contained some information about Dr. Peltz, of course," Nick's father interrupted.

"Yeah, we think so too," Jimmy said. "I mean me, Jimmy, and his mother. So we've made a plan to go to his house here in Apalachicola when we know Dr. Peltz isn't at home, hire a ... whatdoyoucallit ... locksmith and have him open the locked door. And if a safe is inside that office, have him crack that also."

Nick's father laughed, but his mother was serious. "Oh, don't do that, Nick," she said frowning and leaning forward toward him, lit cigarette in hand. "That's dangerous. You shouldn't get involved in this matter at all. What if the police find you in Dr. Peltz's house or, worse yet, in his office, rifling through the doctor's confidential letters. You would go to jail for burglary and robbery."

"I agree. It's a serious risk you don't need to take," Nick's father said. "You are really naïve."

"That's not likely to happen, Dad," Nick said. "We have a good plan. We would do it on a holiday, like the Fourth of July coming up in a couple of weeks, at midday when just about nobody would be walking around town. Jimmy and the locksmith would enter through the back service door, which nobody can see from the street, while I'd be outside across the street to look out for any police or sheriff's deputies that might happen to be cruising around."

"That's ridiculous, Nick," his father, Stephen, said, now looking very annoyed.

"No, Dad, listen," said Nick picking up steam. "If I did spot someone, I would walk up the front steps and ring the bell three times, a sign to the others inside that we may have a problem. I would have my shoulder school bag on me, and if I'm asked what I am doing there, I would just say I am visiting Martha Langston who lives here for one of our tutoring sessions. 'She lives here, and I haven't seen her for quite a while,' ... even though I know she doesn't live there anymore, you see."

"And what if you were then told she doesn't live there?" Stephen asked. Lili turned away in frustrated disbelief and lit another cigarette, her hand shaking.

"I would just say I didn't know that and ask the person where she lives now. I'll need the school bag anyway to carry out any files ... I mean files of interest you know," said Nick with earnest seriousness. "Dad, we have replayed forward every possible scenario."

"Why, you understand that you would be committing a

very serious crime?" Stephen said, with tension in his face now showing. "In any case, none of you know any German!"

"Yeah, well, we took care of that too," Nick countered. "Jimmy's mother found a German locksmith living over in Port St. Joe."

Nick's parents were still angry about this and wanted to dismiss the plot as a figment of the boys' imagination. After all, they knew how fascinated they were with the plots of crime stories.

"The police and the sheriff's office would be all over the place looking for suspects as soon as Dr. Peltz reports that his house and his office were broken into," Lili said. "Don't you realize that?"

"No, Mom," Nick responded again. "There wouldn't be any signs of a break-in. The door locks wouldn't be damaged, the door to his office would be relocked from the inside, the remaining files would appear undisturbed, and the safe would look untouched. It wouldn't be for a very long time in the future that Dr. Peltz might look for one of those files and see it missing. Even then, he wouldn't first think it was stolen."

18

The Heist

The seemingly puerile plan to burglarize Dr. Peltz's home office on the Fourth of July, 1962, was carried out without a hitch, surprising even those involved. A small batch of original documents and letters were smuggled out, selected quickly by Tomas, the German locksmith, as being potentially of interest. They were delivered to Martha in her new house. By now, Martha had completely changed her opinion of Dr. Peltz, having lied to her and finding out about his illegal pharmacy, So the next day, Martha took the papers to the community center in Crawfordville where she had taken her adult education classes and where she still had friends who fondly remembered her. Using the center's mimeograph machine, they helped her make copies of them, a set of which she would give to Rachel.

Tomas and his family had immigrated to the United States in 1933 from a coastal village in Germany; he was only six years old at the time. His father was a fisherman, and so they settled in Port St. Joe in the Florida panhandle where opportunities were plentiful. Tomas later went to technical school to learn to be a locksmith, and his two brothers learned different trades. Their close-knit Protestant family, which had no political inclinations, spoke only German at home, so as Tomas grew up, he became fluent in the language. Martha paid him generously for his critical role in raiding Dr. Peltz's office, and now she paid him well again to try to translate the letters and documents that she received, a job that would take several weeks.

In the meantime, Dr. Peltz was spending less and less time in the Colored Only clinic, only to work with his nurse and Martha every morning to keep close track of his patients who received free medications from the special pharmacy, as he called it, and document their reactions, if any. His nurse agreed these patients required more supervision. Martha didn't understand exactly why, but she was relieved that the doctor's visits became so brief. She had come to dread even seeing him, with his explosive temper, criticizing her at every turn.

A tragic event occurred when one of the younger patients in the Colored Only clinic was reported to have committed suicide by a self-inflicted gunshot. Deaths occurred not infrequently among the oldest and most frail patients in the clinic. While they caused sadness among the staff and other patients, they were seldom shocking. But suicide by a young man was extremely rare in this community. Dr. Peltz himself was visibly shaken and ordered his nurse and Martha to promptly go to the deceased patient's home to find out and record the exact circumstances.

19

Documents in the Safe

Rachel couldn't wait. She had by now become quite engrossed in Dr. Peltz's story. As soon as she received copies of the letters and documents that were taken from Dr. Peltz's safe, which were sent to her by Martha, she paid a German FSU graduate student to translate them for her.

There were letters in both English and German. Many of them turned out to have little if any consequence or were of the kind Hannah Spielman had already mentioned to Martha. The others were curious.

One particular letter exchange over the years stood out as being worth looking into further. They were addressed to a physician named Dr. Hans Wilhelm König in Göttingen, the first one dated June 30, 1943. They were typed on black-bordered stationary with the letterhead *Nationalsozialistische Deutsche Arbeiterpartei*. Below it was Nazi Germany's national emblem, the Imperial Eagle (*Reichsadler*) perched above an encircled swastika. They were signed by Heinrich Himmler, Reichsführer SS,[25] with the salutation

"Herr Doktor König." The text, as translated by the German student, contained the following:

Congratulations on receipt of your doctorate from the University of Göttingen. By the order of the Führer, you are hereby assigned to the Konzentrationslager Auschwitz in Poland.[26] You are directed to arrive there instantly to take up your duties.

In a subsequent letter from Himmler to Dr. König, more specific orders were divulged:

Your assignment is to serve as staff physician of the camp under the direct command of Doktor Josef Mengele, [27] the chief medical officer of the Konzentrationslager Auschwitz and the Zigeunerfamilienlager of the subcamp Birkenau ...

As Rachel read these letters, she wondered who this Doktor König might have been, and why Dr. Peltz would have them. The next series of letters years later, after the war, mostly explained it. The later typed letters were on paper without letterheads, between Dr. Peltz in New York and Dr. König in Colnrade[28] in Lower Saxony, Germany, to which König had escaped indictment for war crimes and crimes against humanity following the war.

Rachel arranged the letters in the order of dates typed on the top lines. Among them was a single opened and empty envelope from König and addressed to Dr. Peltz in Brooklyn, *"Par Avion. By Air Mail,"* postmarked on a Norwegian stamp. And these were some letters between them that were taken from Dr. Peltz's office:

September 10, 1952. My Dear Ernst. I do hope your new position in New York is interesting and gratifying. It must be fascinating to work on top secret medical projects. As for me, I have settled into a quiet private practice in Colnrade, far from the tumult of life in the damned Führer's Germany.

I shall always look back so fondly to our youthful days

in medical school together in beautiful Göttingen. What adventures we had. It was a time of so much excitement and promise in the country. But you, dear Ernst, were fortunate to foresee the future ahead for Jews in Germany and managed to flee to America in time to escape the unspeakable atrocities our countrymen committed against the Jewish people. What we did—yes, myself included—leaves me with everlasting shame. Please do write. Your good friend always, Hans.

October 21, 1952. Dear Hans. It was good to hear from you. You should know that I actually didn't leave Germany until after the war. In the last couple of years of the bloodshed, we lost track of each other in the chaos. I am glad that you now have some insight into the dark side to which you yourself descended in the last years. It was as if a good man like you fell under some mystical, evil spell. I pray that it was against your will and conscience. But now you have apparently become again the real Hans König we all knew. Sincerely, Ernst.

November 1, 1952. My Dear Ernst. Your kind words have helped me so much in my path of penitence. We should meet again, perhaps in New York. Germany still isn't stable enough for you to visit. I do not advise you to do it. The World Congress of Medicine will be held next April in New York. I plan to go. Wouldn't that be a good opportunity for us to reconnect? I hope so. Your good friend always, Hans.

Then there was a small handwritten note on Waldorf Astoria hotel stationary:

April 9, 1953. My Dear Ernst. I made dinner reservations for us at 8:30 at Delmonico's, 2 S. William St. I have a colleague who knows the owner.

And a much later letter among those found from Dr. Peltz to Dr. König:

December 2, 1957. Hans. I want to inform you that I will be leaving New York early next year and moving to Florida to establish a private practice. The government agencies that supported my research here have kindly indicated that I could continue to do some of it in Florida, and they would continue to fund the work if its results were promising. I plan to build a house in a small town called Apalachicola, near the town of Panacea where I will set up my clinical practice. Ernst.

There was also some correspondence in German with a scientist in Germany named Kurt Blome. These had to do with Dr. Peltz working on the CIA-sponsored mind control experiments with Dr. Abramson in New York. Blome was a Nazi war criminal who also experimented on concentration camp prisoners but evaded prosecution after the war. He was recruited by the CIA to work on the secret MK-Ultra program that was based in research facilities at Fort Detrick in Frederick, Maryland. However, he was denied a visa to the United States, so he had to operate from the European Command Intelligence Center in Oberursel, West Germany.

Blome was the supplier of experimental drugs to Abramson and Peltz as well as all the other sites in the United States that were participants in the project. Peltz noted on some of these letters with his own handwriting that he was no friend of Blome; in fact, he detested him and openly deplored his heinous actions in the Holocaust. He must have done this to make it clear to any others who happened to read them in the future that all the correspondence between Peltz and Blome was nothing but "business."

As soon as Rachel had finished analyzing the documents and letters that had been removed from Dr. Peltz's office, her attention turned to finding out more about this man, Hans Wilhelm König, Dr. Peltz's former friend and medical school classmate. She contacted the US National Archives and the Yad Vashem archives in Jerusalem. Security clearance was required at both places before Rachel could speak with anyone there concerning König. She had to complete some elaborate forms with information about herself and the purposes for which she needed information, and they had to be approved by both institutions. She also contacted the German National Library where Rachel was able to talk with an English-speaking staff member who provided her with valuable information about König.

When all the information she could get was obtained, Rachel and her husband, David, invited everyone to their home: Martha Langston and her son, Jimmy, as well as Lili and Stephen Wolff with their son, Nick. They gathered on a beautiful early fall afternoon in 1962 in the small back garden of the Morans' home on Old Augustine Road.

Sitting in lawn chairs, they listened intently to what Rachel had found out.

She read to them the back-and-forth correspondence between Dr. Peltz and his German friend, Dr. Hans Wilhelm König, as they were translated into English.

"So," Rachel began, "this Dr. König was in fact a medical student at the University of Göttingen, just as Dr. Peltz had been. Then they apparently parted ways; Dr. Peltz to America as a Jewish refugee and Dr. König to remain in Germany where he joined the Nazi Party in 1939 and became complicit in the genocide committed. In one of König's letters to Dr. Peltz, he seemed to have misunderstood—just like us—that Dr. Peltz had left Nazi Germany after the war, not before it.

"Then, it appears that this Dr. König decided to join the Waffen-SS in June 1943."

"What's that?" Jimmy asked.

"The Waffen was a combat unit of the Nazi Party," Nick's father replied. "They fought along with the German army and the uniformed police."

"So Dr. König was a Nazi soldier?"

"Not necessarily," said Nick's father. "He could have been a volunteer."

"I did research that question too," said Rachel, "and in fact there is no record of Dr. König having been involved in armed combat."

"But regardless of how he joined," continued Nick's father, "the criminal trials after the war exposed that Waffen units were also very much involved in the atrocities perpetrated against millions—tens of millions—of Jews and other so-called undesirables. Their extermination was what Nazis called the Final Solution."

"Yes," Rachel said. "But that's not all König was involved in. He became a camp doctor at Auschwitz, as I just read to you, and participated in the sadistic selections of hundreds of thousands of victims for the gas chambers as they arrived by trains, crammed into those suffocating cattle cars. And Dr. König reported to Dr. Josef Mengele, the notorious Angel of Death, and actively participated in Mengele's horrific and often fatal experiments with twins."[27]

Suddenly, Rachel stopped. She had tears in her eyes and turned away from the company before she started to sob. Then she abruptly stood up and excused herself for going into the house for a few minutes. David ran after her.

They returned to the yard a little later, Rachel now fully composed. She picked up her comments exactly where she left them off.

"König also worked on behalf of the giant pharmaceutical conglomerate IG Farben, including its subsidiary, Bayer. They were conveniently located near the concentration camp. They had contracts with the Nazi government," Rachel continued. "And König tested drugs those companies made to try on prisoners. Many of them had lethal side effects. It seems that among the Nazi doctors, König had an especially close relationship with the drug companies. He was presumably paid handsomely by them to do their abominable work."[29]

"So what happened to this monster after the war," Martha asked incredulously.

"Well, obviously he survived. According to the German National Library he somehow evaded prosecution and escaped to Colnrade.[28] There he opened a medical practice," Rachel replied.

"The Germans let him do that?" Nick asked.

"Not really. When the authorities found out about it, they reopened the inquest to have him arrested.

"But then he disappeared, never to be seen again. Based on what I found out, my best guess as to his whereabouts would be Sweden, where his wife was born, or maybe Norway. Or possibly he has died," said Rachel.

"But what has this got to do with Dr. Peltz?" wondered Nick's father. "After all, the exchange of letters between Peltz and König that you read to us suggested that they became alienated from each other after the war. It sounds like Dr. Peltz more or less renounced their friendship after he found out about König's role in Auschwitz, ... even though König seemed to express some remorse for his actions in his letters."

"Well," Rachel responded, "maybe it has nothing to do with Dr. Peltz at all. But I still want to find out a little more."

"How?" David asked his wife.

"I want to go to New York for a weekend," Rachel responded, "and meet with a couple of women who survived Auschwitz. Olga Lengyel and Gisella Perl. And perhaps, while I am there, look up Hannah Spielman in Brooklyn, Dr. Peltz's reputedly dead wife."

Martha looked bemused. "I doubt if Hannah would tell you much more that she said to me during her surprise visit to Apalachicola. But go ahead, Rachel; I'll give you her address and telephone number that she gave me when she came to talk with me."

"And what about those other two women?" asked David.

"So Gisella Perl is a Hungarian Jewish gynecologist, like me, who was deported to Auschwitz. She became one of the survivor heroines of the concentration camp. She was tasked with assisting Josef Mengele in the women's camp and to be with him during some of his twisted and cruel experiments on twins.[27, 30, 31] Olga was a surgical assistant in Romania when she was deported to Auschwitz along with her family. She was the only one who survived. After the war she went to New York with plans to create a library dedicated to the Holocaust and human rights in general."

"Do you know them?" David asked again.

"Not Olga, but I have been in touch with her. I knew Gisella, … quite well, in fact. She now works at Mount Sinai Hospital as a highly regarded infertility specialist," Rachel replied.

When the guests left, Rachel commented to David that the others seemed less interested in this matter than she was.

"And you are *more* interested," replied David.

20

Problems in the Colored Only Clinic

By now, Dr. Peltz had stopped seeing patients altogether in the Colored Only office. A month or two earlier he had hired a nurse, an experienced Black woman, to run the clinic. He also hired a new physician, Dr. Michael Stanton, a recent graduate of Mercer University Medical School in Macon, Georgia. Dr. Stanton had just completed his residency in general internal medicine. He was a handsome, blond, and affable young man who quickly and enthusiastically immersed himself in patient care at both clinics.

So now, Dr. Peltz came only in the early mornings to dispense the free medications that were to be given out to certain patients who were scheduled to come in later that day. He no longer needed Martha to help him with the pharmacy logbook; the nurse picked up that task.

From the beginning of her job as Dr. Peltz's assistant, she had to deal with occasional patients who were no-shows, ones who made appointments but didn't keep them. Martha was silently annoyed by this. Now, it became evident to Martha that the previously slow drip of occasional patients who were no-shows was becoming a virtual stream of them, most without an excuse. She also began to observe that a few of the regular and very nice patients were becoming surly, demanding, and short-tempered. *Maybe I was just imagining it*, Martha thought. But even the new nurse commented on it.

When a young woman named Bernadette, one of Martha's favorite patients because of her irrepressible cheerfulness, missed two consecutive visits, she became concerned enough to make a visit to her home after hours. It was nothing much more than a rundown, old cabin. Her mother opened the door and told Martha that Jacqueline had disappeared.

"She just up and left barefooted, her hair uncombed, without saying a word," she said.

Martha was aghast. "How long ago?"

"Oh, maybe a week ago," said Jacqueline's mother, dabbing her tearful eyes with a handkerchief. "Never heard from mah baby since."

"My God, did anyone see her?" Martha asked.

"Yes, an older man who was drivin' north on Route 61 saw her walkin' barefoot on the roadside dirt, toward Wakulla Springs. He said he rolled down the car window and called out to her several times, but she gist kept walkin' without even turning her head."

"Did he report it?"

"Yes, he drove all the way over to Crawfordville to let the Wakulla County Sheriff's Office know. What a nice gentleman."

"And?" Martha asked impatiently.

"Well, by the time the sheriff's men searched the area where she was last seen, even in the woods around there, she was gone."

The next day, the local newspaper, the *Tallahassee Democrat*, reported briefly inside the paper that the body of a young Negro woman was found floating face down in the water of Wakulla Springs. It was Bernadette. The autopsy showed no signs of injury or any foul play. Martha didn't make much of it at first. Martha then put the paper down as tears began to sting her eyes. She saw Bernadette in her mind's eye and thought to herself how unfair it is to lose someone so kind and so young.

21

Weekend in New York

As soon as Rachel landed at Idlewild airport in New York, she took a taxi to Mount Sinai Hospital on the Upper East Side of Manhattan. She went directly to the building where Dr. Gisella Perl's office was located. They had decided to meet there on Saturday afternoon.

An office directory for the building hung on the wall just inside the front doors. Dr. Gisella Perl's office was located on the sixth floor. But another name caught Rachel's eye. On the second floor was the office of Dr. Harold Abramson, with whom Dr. Peltz conducted the CIA-sponsored experiments.

Although they were some thirty years apart in ages, Dr. Perl and Rachel greeted each other like long-lost friends. They hugged and kissed one another's cheeks.

Rachel and Dr. Perl had both overcome tragic events in their lives, and now here they were meeting again in America, two accomplished women practicing medicine in the specialties they each loved, with a freedom from fear they wouldn't have even dared to dream about just fifteen years earlier.

After catching up on each other's lives since they last saw each other, Rachel told Dr. Perl why she was there.

"My husband's general practitioner in Florida is a man named Dr. Ernest Peltz, a Jewish immigrant from Germany. He had settled there just a few years ago and now has a thriving practice with a stellar reputation in the community," Rachel began.

"Ernest Peltz," Dr. Perl interrupted quizzically, "Ernest Peltz, hmmm ... the name is vaguely familiar."

"I believe his former wife, Hannah Spielman, works for you," said Rachel.

"Oh yes, of course; yes, she has worked for me for several years. A good employee."

"I have met her," said Rachel.

"Unfortunately, Hannah is on vacation now ... I suppose with her new husband. So you won't get a chance to see her."

Rachel suddenly connected the dots in her mind. "Before he came to Florida, Dr. Peltz worked right here in this very building, only a few floors below your office. He was a medical researcher with a psychiatrist named Harold Abramson. I just saw Abramson's name on the building directory when I was looking for your office number."

"Ah!" Dr. Perl exclaimed. "Abramson, that's it. I know him. But he is not a psychiatrist, you know. He is an allergist. About as far removed from psychiatry as it can possibly be. But you know, Rachel, I have never met your Dr. Peltz—never even seen him."

Dr. Perl paused to recollect. "Abramson was quite a shady figure, by the way. They were doing some secret research on mind-altering mechanisms and substances. I think it was funded by the Macy Foundation."[22]

"The CIA," said Rachel. "The CIA funded it through the Macy Foundation, the CIA's front."

Dr. Perl looked perplexed.

"Anyway," Rachel continued, "Peltz is a very good doctor but a secretive, peculiar man. Some of us in Tallahassee have even begun to wonder about his past. We found out that he had a German friend from their medical school days who apparently went over to the dark side during the war, joined the Nazi Party Waffen, and was assigned to be a camp doctor in Auschwitz. His name is, ... actually, we don't even know if he is still alive, ... Hans Wilhelm König."

Dr. Perl's face suddenly fell and turned chalk white. She was thunderstruck and speechless for a moment. Frozen in her chair, she swiveled away from Rachel and faced the window behind her desk. Even with her back to her, Rachel noticed Dr. Perl's hands quivering. The silence seemed interminable.

"*Istenem!*" Dr. Perl cried out abruptly in Hungarian as she turned back to Rachel, then in English, "My God!"

"I know König worked with Mengele while he was committing human atrocities in the camp. But do you know more about him?" Rachel asked.

"He was not much better than Mengele," said Dr. Perl. "Dr. König was a monster, much like Mengele. He just tended to follow Mengele's orders. König was Mengele's lackey. I was taken to Auschwitz in 1944, and König came before me in the summer of 1943. I think toward the end, when the Soviet army was already closing in, he was reassigned to a different camp. By then, I myself had been transferred to Bergen-Belsen, the concentration camp in western Germany. So our times at Auschwitz didn't overlap much. But König's notoriety was widely known by the time I arrived."

Gisella Perl then went on to tell Rachel that Dr. König independently conducted electroshock and electroconvulsive experiments on randomly chosen women prisoners, often repeatedly, sometimes twice a week.[31] Mengele sometimes joined him to observe. I know that of the seventy or eighty women who were chosen to be guinea pigs, about thirty died during the experiments.

"And the survivors?" Rachel interrupted.

"Oh, they were all promptly sent to the gas chambers. They were of no use by then," Dr. Perl said sardonically, turning back toward Rachel, appearing red in suppressed anger, pursing her lips, now intensely contacting Rachel's eyes and clenching her jaw.

Rachel's eyes by now were tearing up. But she promptly reassured Dr. Perl that she was all right.

Dr. Perl went on to tell Rachel that Dr. König became closely tied to the IG Farben pharmaceutical conglomerate and especially its subsidiary, Bayer, to test dangerous drugs on female prisoners, some of whom died during those experiments while others suffered horrible side effects like bloody vomiting and painful, bloody diarrhea.

Both Gisella Perl and Rachel were deeply affected and disturbed by this conversation. Holocaust survivors have mostly erased this period of their lives from their memory. So recalling any of it was very painful. Rachel still didn't have any insight into how, if at all, Dr. Peltz might have been indirectly involved in König's activities. She and Dr. Perl embraced tearfully and vowed to keep in touch with each other.

From there, Rachel went to see Olga Lengyel, the other Auschwitz survivor, in her elegant home in Manhattan. They had previously arranged to meet there in the afternoon. To prepare herself for the meeting, Rachel had reread Olga's widely known, graphically detailed book about the horrors of her experience in Auschwitz, published in 1946 only a year after the war ended.[30] Olga was the only one of her family to survive the concentration camps; her husband, parents, and two children perished there.

Olga herself opened the front door of the brownstone house and warmly greeted Rachel, ushering her into the library that was later to become the Memorial Library and Art Collection of the Second World War.

"I must tell you, Ms. Lengyel—" Rachel started.

"Olga, my dear, call me Olga, please."

"Thank you, Olga. I have been a great admirer of yours. Your *Five Chimneys* opened the eyes of much of the civilized world to the barbarism of German Nazis. Now, here you are, devoting yourself to memorializing the Holocaust in your home."

Rachel then introduced herself and told Olga why she was here.

"Yes, I did hear about Dr. König," Olga said. "How could anyone there not hear of him? But he walked in the shadow of Dr. Josef Mengele, who I saw on many occasions, dapper as always, strutting around the camp in his elegant uniform and polished boots. Mengele was always accompanied by an entourage of retainers."

"Did they do you any harm?" Rachel asked, suddenly cupping her mouth with tears running down her cheeks.

"Not me personally. Mengele was only interested in twins to experiment on. And I don't know how König selected women for his electroshock experiments. But as a member of the infirmary staff, I was a witness to the inhumane treatment of the sick inmates and even some of the horrifying experiments that the doctors did gleefully."

The conversation led to Olga's knowledge of König's fate.

"He was transferred to another camp, I can't remember which one, before Auschwitz was liberated. I really don't know the details, but apparently he escaped before he could be arrested for prosecution as a war criminal. He had the chutzpah to open a practice in a remote German village, can you believe it! And then he disappeared. Some said he died in one of the Scandinavian countries."

"One last question," Rachel said. "Do you happen to know about a German doctor named Ernest ... or Ernst ... Peltz? He came to set up a practice in North Florida a few years ago and endeared himself quickly to the people in the region. We found out that Dr. Peltz was a friend of König. In fact, they were medical school classmates together."

"The name is not familiar," replied Olga.

"How can I find out what if any role Dr. Peltz had in the Holocaust and Auschwitz particularly," asked Rachel.

"Oh, I think that can be easy, my dear. Because of my book and my project here, I have access to all the key archives concerning the Holocaust. It may take a bit of time, but I'll be happy to help you with that."

Before Rachel left New York, she found out that Hannah was no longer living in Brooklyn. She had gotten remarried to an older businessman and moved into an apartment on the seventeenth floor of the upscale San Remo on Central Park West between Seventy-Fourth and Seventy-Fifth Streets, adjacent to Central Park. When the taxi dropped Rachel off at the address, she looked up at the magnificent Renaissance Revival architecture of the building. Its mere size was awe-inspiring. A courteous doorman escorted her in, called up to make sure the guest was expected, and led her to the elevator.

Hannah graciously but cautiously greeted Rachel. Entering the apartment, Rachel was struck by the immense Turkish carpets, framed by what must have been recently glossed and now shining mahogany flooring. Antique furniture prevailed. Rachel was particularly captivated by the large windows from which the vista of Central Park and the city's skyline were on view.

"You know, Rachel, I wasn't remarried yet when I went down to Florida to meet with Martha. But by that time, I had met a wonderful older Jewish gentleman, a widower, who just happened to be an executive vice president for strategic investment at a Wall Street firm," said Hannah as they sank into plush armchairs facing each other, separated by a glass-covered coffee table. Hannah had arranged dishes on it filled with scones, jams, and finger sandwiches, as well as cups.

Hannah stood up and brought in two steaming pots. "Coffee or tea?" she asked, holding both pots up, one after the other.

"Coffee, please."

"So as I was saying," Hannah continued, "I can't complain about my situation now. My parents fled from their destroyed village in Russia during the pogroms, ... and now," as she wiped her eyes, "look at this!" Hannah swept her arm broadly to encompass the room and the view from the windows.

"Would I be able to meet your husband?" Rachel asked meekly.

"He is away this weekend," Hannah replied, "on an important business trip."

"So, Hannah," Rachel said, "may I call you Hannah?"

"Certainly, my dear."

"Martha has told me the story of your relationship with your former husband," Rachel continued.

"She couldn't have told you everything," Hannah interrupted.

"As Martha may have told you, Dr. Peltz now has a thriving practice, and frankly he has become quite beloved by the community. But his behavior over the past year or so seems to several of us to have changed. Much changed. And I've heard that even some of his patients have become concerned about it."

"What is he doing?" Hannah asked.

"Well, it's hard to describe if you are not there. He has lost much of his warmth and interest in his patients. For Martha and others on his staff, he has become quickly irritable ... and he sometimes even berates Martha loudly in front of the patients if he thinks she has made a mistake."

"Hmm," Hannah mumbled as she put her finger on her lips.

Is it possible that she has an ever-so-subtle, roguish smile on her face? Rachel thought to herself.

"You mean he has become bossy? Forceful, maybe even commanding?"

"Well, I suppose so, ... but certainly not all the time," Rachel replied. "But of course I have only seen him twice myself, and we didn't even talk to each other on either of those occasions. But I have no reason not to believe Martha and the others."

"Well, what do you know!" Hannah, shouted with a contemptuous smile, raising her arms and standing up momentarily. "That's my Ernst! Exactly!" Hanna yelled.

Rachel was startled by Hanna's shrillness. *What an annoying, sarcastic, and pompous woman she is,* Rachel said to herself.

"We raided the safe in his house while he was away, just like you tried to do when you were living together in Brooklyn," continued Rachel, "and we found some letters back and forth between Dr. Peltz and another German doctor named Hans Wilhelm König. Have you ever heard of him?"

"Of course," said Hannah. "Ernst was almost obsessed with him. They had been good friends since medical school, as far as I know, but they became alienated from each other many years ago. Ernst could barely contain his outrage at König's role in the Holocaust. He found out that König had been a camp doctor at Auschwitz during the war, working alongside that barbaric Angel of Death, Josef Mengele. Not just assisting Mengele, mind you, in his sadistic 'experiments' on twins but doing some experiments on his own, ... on the brains of women prisoners, no less."[31]

"I see."

"And as time passed, Ernst became increasingly infuriated as he recalled all the evil König had done. He flew into outbursts of unhinged rage at times, castigating himself for ever having become König's friend. And that's when I would have to quickly leave our apartment in Brooklyn, ... because I couldn't take it any longer."

"My God," Rachel gasped. "Didn't he see a psychiatrist for this?"

"Hah!" Hannah raised her piercing voice. "I once suggested it, and he came at me with outreached arms, appearing like he wanted to strangle me."

No sooner had Rachel returned home from New York, there was a message from Gisella Perl, wanting to speak with her. It was now Sunday night, and she was much too exhausted to call her back then. But the next morning, she returned the call from her office.

"Hello, Gisella," she said, "I hadn't expected to hear from you so soon. It was a very productive weekend for me, and it was such an honor and delight to see you again."

"Listen," Gisella said in a hurried voice. "I have done all the research you asked me to do. My friends and colleagues at the different archives did all the searching yesterday, yes, on a Sunday. They all got back to me promptly. The bottom line is that there is not a trace of Dr. Ernst or Ernest Peltz to be found anywhere. As you know, fortunately for us at least now, those German Nazis were obsessed with documenting every detail, precisely listing all the names, without exception, and what each individual did in the concentration camps," Gisella sighed audibly, "your Dr. Peltz simply doesn't seem to exist in the records."

"That's a relief. At least we know now that he himself wasn't involved in any way in that merciless, horrific Holocaust. I would have been shocked if an observant Jewish person had done anything abhorrent at Auschwitz. Thank you so much, Gisella."

As she put down the phone, Rachel thought, *How frustrating this has been! The real truth still lies hidden. But I can't give up now!*

22

Dr. Peltz's Pharmacy

Meanwhile, Martha was becoming increasingly concerned about the strange behavior of some of the regular patients in the Colored Only clinic. They were people she had gotten to know well but were now seemingly changed somehow. There had been three unexpected deaths over the past few months that were especially troubling. It crossed Martha's mind that perhaps the medications that were being dispensed from the free pharmacy might have something to do with it. When she notified Dr. Peltz about these events and encounters, he was clearly annoyed by even the suggestion that these charitable medications might have been the cause.

"You have got to get these muddled thoughts out of your head," he snapped angrily at her, "and get back to concentrating on your real responsibilities."

"May I ask what's in these pills?" Martha asked sheepishly.

"*No* you may *not!*" bellowed Dr. Peltz. Then, pulling himself together, he said, "but you might as well know before you cause more trouble. They are very mild sedative pills. They have no side effects. And I give them only to selected anxious patients to improve the quality of their already wretched lives." He then abruptly waved Martha away.

When she went back to her desk, there was little activity in the clinic, so she started mulling over what had been said. *Something is very wrong here, I just know it. But I can't connect the dots. I have to think more clearly because I must be missing something.*

Finally, she realized what she had to do. She knew where the keys to the medication cabinets were kept in Dr. Peltz's desk. So she began by examining the pill containers from which they were dispensed. Their labels were all marked by that single pharmacy in Frederick, Maryland, from which they came, named "BLUEBIRD Apothercary, FDC." The names of the labeled drugs were "LysAS, SDZ" and "LysAS, LIL," "PSILOSDZ" and "PSILO, LIL," "Tetrahydrol," "Lys-Tetrahydrol," and "PB," each color-coded for different doses.[32]

Martha also knew the location of the large logbook Dr. Peltz kept in a locked drawer—and the place where the key was kept to open it. Entering the names of the patients who received the medications had been, after all, one of Martha's responsibilities when she first started working in the clinic, so she was familiar with the notations written for each patient: name and medical diagnosis, dose of the medication, start date, discontinuation date (if the drug was stopped), dose changes, patient-reported side effects, and clinical correlates. For some patients, the letter "P" was substituted for the medication name and dose. She didn't know what that stood for.

Martha spent evenings poring over the logbook entries, taking notes, and trying to find correlations with individual patient diagnoses. It finally became clear to her that all the patients who she thought had acted strangely or died were, in fact, listed in the medication logbook. They had taken the medications Dr. Peltz dispensed. There were some other names listed, of course, in whom there were no apparent changes. She called Rachel to ask for advice.

"I had no idea that Dr. Peltz was distributing unknown drugs at no cost to some of his patients!" Rachel was stunned and appalled. "He certainly wasn't asking for their consent to do so if they were research subjects, and I bet most of these poor people were too afraid to ask him what they contained!"

"Dr. Peltz reluctantly told me they were mild antianxiety pills. Do you think they were something else?" Martha asked.

"I can't even imagine, Martha. But if their personality changes occurred as you described them, they surely wouldn't have been sedative pills, and whatever else they contained couldn't have been anything good."

"And what do you think the P stands for? One vial of drugs is labeled with only a P, whatever that is."

"The P probably stands for placebo. A blank. Something that is used in clinical research trials of drugs as a control, ... sort of like a sugar pill," Rachel replied.

"Do you think I should report this?" Martha asked.

"Of course, but let me call you back after I think about how and where you should report it," replied Rachel.

A few minutes later, she called back.

"The first step would be the Florida Board of Medicine. And you know what? Dr. Houston Calhoun—yes, the same one who clashed with Dr. Peltz—is now chairman of its board. I'll talk to him first."

Rachel found Dr. Calhoun to be more than receptive—perhaps even pleased—to take on this case. Rachel, with Martha's help, arranged for Dr. Calhoun to make a personal visit to the clinics in Panacea on a weekend when they knew Dr. Peltz would be away. She and Martha could then show the curiously eager Dr. Calhoun around. Only the Colored Only clinic had the "complimentary" drug dispensary. And only the Colored Only clinic had a detailed logbook documenting which patients were taking which drugs and at what doses. Their entries were accompanied by meticulous notes concerning any clinical consequences, mostly using nebulously abbreviated words or undecipherable acronyms.

Dr. Calhoun said he would promptly file a complaint with the board and ask for the case to be investigated.

Rachel was appalled. *Was this man really continuing that sham research with mind-altering drugs he had done in New York before moving here? Was he really transporting unlicensed drugs across state lines—and then distributing them to unknowing patients without their consent? This is not only unethical; it's downright illegal!*

Less than two weeks later, agents from the board came to the Colored Only clinic to meet with Dr. Peltz. They demanded that he hand over all the pills in their respective containers. Dr. Peltz threw a fit, even lapsing into German.

"Then how do you expect me to help these sick patients?" Dr. Peltz protested, his face flushed and contorted.

"Oh, come on now, Dr. Peltz, you know very well how to manage them without these drugs. You do it with the White patients, don't you?"

Dr. Peltz was enraged, but he knew he had to comply if he didn't want to have his medical license revoked. The cabinets were cleared of the drugs, which were placed in secure, labeled containers to be taken to a certified laboratory. Chemical analysis soon showed that they contained some form of lysergic acid, LSD, cannabis, phenoperidine, or some combination of these, along with others that couldn't be identified, while some of them contained only an inert compound.

The chemists concluded that the inert compound must have been a placebo.

Dr. Peltz's medical license was suspended while the matter was investigated further, but that didn't stop him from continuing to practice. The case was advanced from the state up to the US Bureau of Narcotics and Dangerous Drugs.[33] Shortly thereafter, FBI agents came down from Washington to seize all the drugs, samples of other drugs that appeared to be improperly labeled, the logbook, and any other materials that could be implicated in pursuing the case.

It was soon discovered that Dr. Peltz was indeed continuing the experiments he had conducted with Dr. Harold Abramson as part of the covert MKUltra program of the CIA to develop new mind-altering drugs.[22] Now he was continuing the experiments on the Black patients in Panacea. The drugs used were supplied by that pharmacy in Frederick, Maryland, which was just a front for MKUltra projects. The research sites had now spread beyond academic medical centers and universities to local private practice physicians in rural areas, like Panacea, where the experiments came under even less oversight.

Martha was angry. This was the last straw for her working with Dr. Peltz. He had been exposed as a possible criminal, exploiting a vulnerable population of impoverished Black people and knowingly putting them at great risk of their lives. She started to feel heart-broken about being herself an unwitting accessory to Peltz's operation. And she was ashamed of herself for agreeing to this man's order to write those notes in his logbook, identifying each subject. She called Rachel to get her thoughts about other job opportunities.

"Well, why don't you come here?" Rachel asked, to Martha's great surprise.

"What do you mean?"

"I am part of a group practice of some very good—and ethical—physicians in Tallahassee who work in other specialties. We are looking for a head practice manager to oversee a pretty complex medical practice."

"Oh, Rachel, I am not at all qualified for that," replied Martha.

"It comes with a very nice salary, you know," said Rachel, switching into recruitment mode.

"But I am not qualified—"

"Nonsense!" Rachel interrupted. "I can't think of anyone better."

"But—"

"Our physicians would like to meet you. I'm sure they will think likewise. We will schedule you for meetings with them in Tallahassee."

"When?"

"Now! This week! Get ready to take a day or two of sick leave to come up here. We'll put you up in a hotel overnight if we need two days."

Martha was expeditiously hired. She gave Dr. Peltz two weeks' notice and put her house up for sale. During this time, she was able to say goodbye to most of the patients she had come to love in the Colored Only clinic. Many tears were shed, and hugs were exchanged. She reassured them that Dr. Stanton was a very fine physician who was up-to-date on the latest developments in medicine. And to some, she said she wanted to keep in touch, which provoked even more tears and hugs.

23

The Young Detectives

Nick's parents had dropped bits and pieces of the evolving story to him in casual conversation at dinner. Nick's curiosity about Dr. Peltz now seemed to know no bounds. He, with Jimmy, conspired to do more "detective work" and "spying" about him, pretentiously assuming the roles of Sherlock Holmes and James Bond, respectively. Just for the adventure of it.

Before Rachel went for the weekend in New York, she had given Nick and Jimmy permission to go to her house and have her husband show them all the *original, untranslated* letters that were exchanged between Dr. Peltz and his former friend, the shady Dr. Hans Wilhelm König. She had told her husband, David, to expect them, and she placed the letters in a pile on her desk, pleading with the boys not to crease them, stain them, or write anything on them.

So on that Sunday afternoon, Nick and Jimmy went to Rachel's house. David let them in and gave them the pile of letters to work on at the cleaned kitchen table. He had even bought them two pairs of white gloves to wear when handling the letters. The boys arranged the letters into two columns, the first had the ones written by König, running down the table in chronological sequence, and in the second column were Dr. Peltz's letters next to each letter in response to König. They noted that the letters from Dr. Peltz were all on vintage yellowed typing paper and those from König were on onion skin typing paper. David was too curious to not join them.

After half an hour of intensely perusing the letters, all three of them were stumped.

"Well, it looks like Dr. Peltz felt animosity toward König from the very outset," said Jimmy. But that didn't contribute anything new to the case.

Examining the letters again, Nick bent down to look at them more closely. And then, without moving his head or position, he asked David, "Sir, do you by chance have a magnifying glass?"

"Sure," replied David, and he went to get it. Now, with his handheld magnifying glass, Nick bent down even further, nose almost touching the letters, and scanned each line of every letter, first one from König and then the corresponding response from Peltz, in chronologic order, from the initial correspondence to the last.

"Something is peculiar here," Nick muttered without raising his head. Then he stood up straight. "Yes, look with the magnifying glass, both of you."

Jimmy and David did that, one after the other, but they still didn't see anything peculiar.

"Look at the characters of the letters. Letters from both of them were typed on old manual typewriters, like a Smith Corona or a Remington. And most of these vintage machines had unique faults. What did they used to call them … idiosyncrasies. See, for example, this letter from König," as Nick pointed to it. "The lowercase letter *t*, wherever it appears, is always slipped ever-so-slightly below the line. And look, the letter *o* is consistently smudged in the middle throughout the page. And look here. The capital letters *H* and *Y* are always followed by the rest of the word following an inadvertently half-skipped space."

Nick kept looking for more idiosyncrasies. "And these faults appeared in *all* the letters from *both* König and Peltz," he said without looking up. "And they all have one-inch margins."

"I suppose then that they were both using the same brand of typewriters," concluded David.

"It would be a crazy coincidence. What made you think of this?" Jimmy asked Nick.

"Sherlock Holmes," replied Nick, looking up at last, grinning from ear to ear.

"Yeah, right, Sherlock Holmes now reincarnated as Nick Wolff!" said Jimmy mockingly.

"No, I am serious, Jimmy. In *A Case of Identity*, one of my favorite stories, Holmes solves the mystery of a missing person by studying the typewriter idiosyncrasies in typed letters from someone else.[34] Really. So even if they happened to be using the exact same make of typewriters, the idiosyncrasies are unique to each individual machine."

"That's not possible," said David shaking his head in continued disbelief. "Are you trying to say, Nick, that *all* these letters were written on the same typewriter?"

24

Identities Revealed

David informed Rachel what the boys found in the original letters from Dr. Peltz's home office. She didn't appear shocked at all. She met with Martha, but Martha had already heard about it from her son, Jimmy.

"What does this mean?" Martha asked.

"It means, Martha, that Dr. Peltz must have typed *all* these letters himself, using different kinds of typing paper for his own letters and for the ones he wanted people to believe were König's."

"Why would he do such a thing?"

"Probably to use them in his own defense—in case it ever became necessary—to show beyond doubt that Peltz himself had nothing to do with the Nazi Party or with the Holocaust, but König did. He wanted to—"

Martha was now confused. "Do you mean ... are you saying that ..."

"Yes," Rachel replied, "I am saying that Dr. Peltz and Dr. König were one and the same person. I've been suspecting that for quite some time but didn't want to tell any of you until I was sure. This by itself isn't enough to prove it, but I've had other reasons to be certain that their identities were the same."

"Jesus!" Martha blurted out. "Do you realize, Rachel, ..." as her eyes welled with tears, "that I've lived with and ... and worked for a Nazi?

"A Nazi *war criminal*, yes," replied Rachel.

"But he is Jewish ..."

After a pause, Rachel replied, "How do you know?"

Now that Martha was working in Tallahassee, managing the group practice Rachel belonged to, they saw each other practically every day. So they often took a break together in the lunchroom. They were now both eager to discuss what to do with Dr. Peltz's situation.

"Should we let him know that we are now pretty sure he is Dr. König?" Martha asked.

"Certainly not," snapped Rachel emphatically. "We don't really have any independent proof. And we haven't even contacted the authorities yet. I've got to find out where to start. This must stay strictly amongst us for now. If Dr. Peltz even sensed that he was being suspected of it, he would disappear instantaneously. Never to be seen again."

"So how strong is your own feeling that he really *is* König?" Martha asked.

Rachel's response came unexpectedly and without hesitation.

"As I said, I am certain of it!"[35]

"How?" asked Martha, stunned.

"I have now seen photos of König from his time in the Auschwitz concentration camp, attired in Nazi uniform, boots and all. They are unmistakably Dr. Peltz, and ..."

After a moment of silence, Martha said, "... and what?"

Rachel hesitated and looked distracted. "Ummm, … nothing really."

"So what would happen to Dr. Peltz if he was arrested and found to be a Nazi war criminal?" Martha asked.

"Most likely nothing. He would be let go eventually," Rachel replied. "You know, only a very small number of Nazi war criminals who managed to get into the United States after the war have been deported back to Germany, or whatever country in Europe they came from, and prosecuted there. And only a few of those prosecuted abroad were sentenced to prison. Fewer yet, *if any at all*, were executed."

"My God, these people haven't even had to atone for their sins," Martha said, dismayed.

Suddenly, Rachel's mien turned dark.

"Martha, look at me," she said, pulling her chair closer to her and peering into her eyes. "Dr. Peltz is a *fraud*."

"What's that word, *fraud*?"

"It means that he is dishonest. He is a damned liar and an imposter. Martha, however kindly you looked up to him at the beginning—"

"Surely not anymore," Martha interrupted.

"…. He was and *still is* an evil man," Rachel finished.

Horrified, Martha asked: "And he will never be punished for it?"

"That would be very, very wrong, wouldn't it?" Rachel replied sardonically.

25

Passover

Monday, April 8, marked the first day of Passover in 1963. This is the major Jewish holiday that celebrates the biblical story of the Israelites' flight from slavery in ancient Egypt. A communal Passover seder, the ritual feast, was scheduled to start at sundown in the Social Hall of Temple Israel in Tallahassee. By the afternoon of the event, dozens of mostly women members of the congregation were hard at work preparing the elaborate dishes to be served in long-established ritual courses throughout the long evening. Rachel was one of them, as she had been in previous years. She had closed her practice at noon that day. Rachel brought Martha along as her guest, obtaining the rabbi's permission in advance. The rabbi even gave her permission to join Rachel in the kitchen to observe the preparation of the seder courses but not participate in it.

Rachel and Martha chattered away in the kitchen, mostly about the seder rituals and traditions. But they occasionally lowered their voices so that the women working at the other table would not hear them. The women there were talking loudly with each other and every now and then threw suspicious glances toward Rachel and Martha. They knew Rachel but had never seen Martha. Silently, a girl in her preteens, dressed for the occasion, snuck up beside Martha and looked up at her, smiling. She wanted to watch Rachel at work.

"What's your name?" Rachel asked.

"Sarah," the girl replied, "and that's my Mami over there, in that dark brown dress." As the girl pointed toward her, Mrs. Feldman put down her utensils and looked up with a ferocious frown toward Rachel and Martha.

Rachel turned to Martha, speaking even more quietly than before.

"Are you talking about Dr. Peltz?" the girl Sarah interrupted, still by the women's side.

"Why, yes …" Rachel hesitated. "We have been talking about what a nice man he is."

"He is really nice," said Sarah. "I know he is here tonight. He is my mother's doctor, you know."

Sarah now wandered away, her curiosity apparently satisfied. She returned to stand next to Mrs. Feldman, a heavyset, dour woman with deep wrinkles on her face. Mother and daughter engaged in a heated conversation, with Sarah frequently glancing at Martha and Rachel. Mrs. Feldman then took her daughter aside, appearing quite animated.

The rabbi looked into the kitchen, stepped forward, and thanked all the women for their work.

The Wolff family, including Jimmy, arrived early, as did Dr. Peltz. Seats were not assigned, so Dr. Peltz asked the Wolffs to join him at the most conspicuous round table in the hall, the one closest to the stage and right in front of the lectern. In fact, he staked out a seat for himself that turned his back to the stage but faced the congregation that was filtering in. He wanted to make sure everybody knew he was here.

Rachel, David, and their guest, Martha, had seats at the same table, although Rachel spent most of the evening running back and forth from the kitchen, helping to serve the many ritual courses of the seder.

The rabbi started by reciting the *Kiddush* blessing at the podium; candles were lit, and the first cups of wine were served to each congregant. This was followed by ritual hand-washing by everyone with clear water poured over both hands from a vessel into a bowl at each table setting. Rachel and the other volunteers now brought out the first course, as mandated, which used individual specially made seder platters with samples of several vegetables arrayed around the indented compartments for each of them, encircling the central depression of the platters. The vegetables included parsley, celery, Romaine lettuce, and two especially bitter but required herbs, uncooked maror and haroset. These were intended to remind the diners of the bitterness of slavery. Samples of the vegetables could be dipped into a cup of saltwater, symbolizing the tears shed by the Israelites. Rachel herself brought the dishes to Dr. Peltz's table on a large tray; she served the doctor first.

The ceremony would continue for several hours, following a well-established sequence of wine tasting, blessings, prayers, and songs. Bitter maror was also served as a separate course at a later point, to be eaten sandwiched between two pieces of matzo, while listening to readings from the story of Exodus.

Dr. Peltz looked unusually subdued and distracted from the moment he arrived. Rachel, David, and the Wolffs attributed this to the ongoing investigation into his pharmacy, which only they knew about at this point. At about nine o'clock, well after the seder platters had been consumed, Dr. Peltz abruptly stood up and, without excusing himself, hurried to the men's room. He stayed there for quite a while. When he returned to the table, he looked ashen. He feebly smiled at the others and apologized for his absence. Before he sat down, he said he had to make an urgent phone call, presumably to one of his patients, and left again.

"I am all right," he said, finally sitting back down. "Just a bit of indigestion."

But then, a few minutes later, he suddenly doubled over in pain, shoving his chair away from the table, and bending over his knees with arms crossed, loudly groaning, *"Oh mein Gott!"* Dr. Peltz had dry heaves.

Rachel, still serving dishes, was taken aback by seeing Mrs. Feldman with Dr. Peltz on a chair she had drawn up next to him. She was with her husband this time. As soon as she saw Rachel bringing a tray, she stood up to leave.

"Wait a minute, Mrs. Feldman," Dr. Peltz said, raising his index finger. He searched his trouser pockets for a piece of paper, took out his pen and, with a trembling hand, wrote something to give to her.

As Mrs. Feldman left, Rachel placed the dishes at the table, and, as she left to go back to the kitchen, David stood up and grabbed her arm.

"Rachel, look at Dr. Peltz," he said. "He looks really sick. What should we do?"

"Nah," Rachel replied dismissively. "It's probably just something he ate. He will be fine." She hurried back to the kitchen.

Dr. Peltz tried to stand up, teetering and wobbling, needing to grasp the back of his chair. He was perspiring profusely and then suddenly bent over again in agony.

When Professor Wolff asked him whether he would like him to call out for a doctor in the hall, Dr. Peltz practically lunged at him and yelled *"Absolut nicht! Du must nicht!"* It sounded like a command.

"What's the matter, Dr. Peltz?" David asked.

"I don't feel well at all. Tremendous pain in abdomen. Colic. I had diarrhea, and that eased the pain a bit but only for a few minutes. And now my vision has become blurry. I am seeing haloes when I look up at the lights."

A small crowd was beginning to gather around the table. The rabbi also came over, very concerned, as did Rachel finally. She bent down to speak into Dr. Peltz's ear.

"Dr. Peltz," Rachel said loudly, "I am going to call for an ambulance right now to take you to TMH. They'll figure out what this is and how to make you feel more comfortable."

Dr. Peltz looked up into Rachel's eyes.

"Absolutely not! Get away from here! I am already beginning to feel better, and I just want to go home to sleep it off," he said sternly.

"You are a stubborn man," Rachel replied. "I will drive you home. You are in no condition to drive. David will follow us. Can you give me your keys?"

Dr. Peltz searched in his pockets with coarsely shaking hands, partly standing up.

"Here. My car keys. Red Chrysler Coupe," as he handed them to her, "and here is the house key," from the other hand.

Dr. Peltz was supported out of the building. Rachel found the car and opened the passenger side door. With some difficulty, the doctor was placed into the passenger seat. He didn't notice Martha sliding into the back seat.

26

Is He Dead?

David followed closely in his own car. He would be needed to help get Dr. Peltz into his house. As Rachel drove in the dark, well above the speed limit, she kept one eye on Dr. Peltz who was now slouched in his seat, head bowed. He seemed to be lapsing in and out of consciousness. He was still moaning, but the sound was more muffled now.

Half-way to Apalachicola, Dr. Peltz became silent and appeared to have stopped breathing. Rachel quickly pulled over to the side of the road, yanked him out of his seat with Martha's assistance and dragged him to the edge of a roadside grassy field. There, Rachel started to pump his chest to resuscitate him. Trailing behind, David also pulled over and got out of his car.

It was pitch dark, and the road had been empty, but then a car heading in the same direction slowed down. Someone from inside the car asked if they needed help.

"No, thanks," shouted David. "Everything is under control."

Dr. Peltz started to breathe again. The three of them

hauled him back to the car and struggled to put him back into the passenger seat.

"Stick with the plan," Rachel said to Martha as they resumed the drive, gasping for air after her effort.

David looked at his watch: it was 11:00 p.m. There was a full moon, which made transferring the doctor from his car into his house a bit easier. But the task was much more strenuous than they had imagined. They had to prop him up under both arms, dragging his legs behind him. Taking him up the front steps required David to also lift him by the ankles, with the women holding him up by his arms.

Once inside, Martha turned on the lights with her free elbow. They decided there would be no way they could carry Dr. Peltz upstairs to his bedroom. So Martha led the way to one of the guest bedrooms at the back of the house on the ground floor where she herself slept during the time she lived here. They lifted his limp body onto the bed.

Turning on his side by himself, Dr. Peltz startled them by moaning loudly and mumbling almost incoherently something about feeling better and wanting to be left alone to sleep it off and get back to work early in the morning.

"Well, I'll be damned," said Rachel.

Relieved, David said he would drive Dr. Peltz's car back to Tallahassee to the temple's parking lot and leave the ladies to care for the doctor. Martha and Rachel sat in the living room, alternately taking turns to check on how Dr. Peltz was doing. There was not much to do for him as he now appeared to be sleeping soundly.

They talked about what to do now under these circumstances. They went over how they would complete their mission. From inside the room where Dr. Peltz was lying, Rachel thought she heard him speaking in a low voice, slurring his words. There were long pauses in between, almost as if he was on a phone call.

Someone outside the house was trying to unlock the front door. Alarmed, Martha and Rachel jumped to their feet. The door opened before they could get there, and Hunter Langston appeared.

"What's going on?" Hunter asked.

"Well, what are *you* doing here then?" Martha exclaimed.

"I'm thuh doctor's housekeeper, yawl know. I tuh look into any suspicious activity that goes on hare. Yawl know that, Martha," Hunter replied. "Is thuh doctor in trouble?"

"Yes, Hunter," Martha said. "I'm afraid he is very sick. Maybe even dying. He got sick at the dinner tonight."

"You're Rachel, right?" Hunter turned to Rachel. "Aren't yawl uh doctor too? So why can't yawl do anything?"

Hunter assumed a protective, possessive tone that Martha hadn't seen from him before. He then walked into the room where Dr. Peltz was laid and closed the door behind him. From the living room, Martha and Rachel could hear some talking behind the door, but they couldn't make out the words.

Hunter came out holding a piece of paper, which he folded and stuffed into his blue jeans pocket.

"Yawl look after him, hear?" Hunter said as he left the house.

Around 2:00 a.m., it was Martha's turn to look in on Dr. Peltz. But this time she ran right back to the living room and shook Rachel awake.

"Rachel! Rachel! He stopped breathing again! He stopped making those sounds."

Rachel sprung to her feet to examine him. He was unarousable. When the lights in the room were turned on, he did indeed appear dead.

"Now we have to do as we had planned. And we must do it before sunrise," said Rachel, "so there's no time to waste."

Rachel stayed by the bedside for a few minutes and mumbled something Martha didn't understand.

"*Yitgadat v'yitkadash sh'mei raba b'alma di-v'ra.*"[36]

The two women lifted Dr. Peltz out of the bed and placed him in a body bag Rachel had bought and kept in the trunk of her car for this occasion. Not bothering with the zipper, they carried the body down the small hill using the riveted handles on the sides of the bag, toward the dock where the boat was tied. Martha knew the way. She had gone there many times. Every now and then, some distant shouts and bursts of laughter could be heard from the direction of Hunter's house in the nearby woods, where all the lights were still on.

"That's Hunter and his buddies starting off another wild weekend of drinking and partying," Martha whispered.

Rachel crossed her closed lips with her index finger and shook her head vigorously to remind Martha that not a sound was to be made.

Dr. Peltz's body in the open bag was lifted into the center of the boat with some difficulty. Martha turned on the engine to warm it up, shifted it forward to idling speed, and then cast off the lines.

About fifty miles offshore, the boat was slowed down and then idled in gear. They thought they might have heard a creak from the boat where the body was lying. Looking down at it, it seemed to slide somewhat sideways.

"Just the waves," said Martha.

Without much ceremony, Martha and Rachel together pushed the body overboard.

Returning to the shore, still in the dead of night, both women were overcome with relief. The job was done, and they sat back in their seats for a while, exhausted. They wanted to relax, but it was not to be.

27

Stars of the Night

At a distance, Martha spotted a tiny, solitary, flashing blue light and pointed at it. Fixing their eyes in that direction, they realized that it was coming their way at a high speed. A searchlight from it suddenly appeared. Martha slowed the boat down to cruising speed. The approaching vessel was a small US Coast Guard patrol boat, no more than one hundred feet in length. Not far behind it was an old fishing vessel, well lighted, with what appeared to be several men on board. As the Coast Guard patrol boat pulled up alongside Dr. Peltz's motorboat, a crew member ordered Martha through a megaphone to idle the boat so that the two men could step into it. The coast guardsmen identified themselves and then, without saying anything more, searched the inside of the boat with flashlights. One of them saw a small object under the back seat, inspected it, shook his head and shrugged his shoulders, and then placed it in his pocket. His partner saw something else and did likewise.

Turning to Martha and Rachel, the captain and his right hand began to interrogate them.

"What are you two ladies doin' by yourselves in this little boat in the middle of the night in the Gulf? Y'all know you are more than fifty miles offshore?"

"We must have lost track of the distance. Are we doing something illegal, officer?" Rachel asked. "We're just unwinding from a hectic week at work ... and gazing up at the bright full moon and the glimmering stars."

"Nothing wrong or illegal that I know of, ma'am. We got orders from our superior over at the base in Panama City to come here at full speed to look around hereabouts," replied the coast guardsman. Which of y'all is the pilot of this boat?"

"Me." Martha raised her hand.

"Do you own it?" the captain asked.

"No, sir." Martha responded. "It's owned by a good friend and my former boss who has kindly allowed me to use it."

"This is all kinda unusual, y'all understand." the captain said. "I need to see the boat registration, proof of ownership, and proofs of identity from both of you."

"The registration stickers are on both sides of the bow," Martha said as she started searching for the official documents in the boat's dashboard glove compartment next to the steering wheel. After flipping through unrelated papers, she found them and handed them over. Rachel and Martha gave the men their driver's licenses.

"Mind if we sit down to study these?" the right hand asked.

"Sure," replied Martha, "anywhere you wish."

The two coast guard patrolmen then spent considerable time silently writing up the information, one of them holding a flashlight and the other scribbling, as the boat gently and quietly rocked in place.

Not far away now, Martha and Rachel could see the old fishing boat. As the boat was well lit, the women could see the fishermen casting out nets, around the same area where they first spotted the coast guard vessel.

"So the owner of this here boat is this man, Ernest Peltz, right?"

"Yeah," replied Martha. "*Doctor* Ernest Peltz."

"Where is he now?"

"Oh, he is not at his home right now, ..." Martha hesitated. "He is away in New York. He goes there, you know, every weekend to do his medical research."

"Everything seems to be in order," said the captain, "but dad-gummit, I still think something is amiss here. I will have to let you go this time after we've accompanied you back to the dock."

Martha asked the coast guard officers what the fishing boat behind them was doing.

"Ma'am," the captain said, "we see them all the time when we are on patrol. Some of these boats are docked near where we are stationed in Panama City, and they come out here at night to do some really good deep-sea fishing. They often follow us to get a good catch. Nighttime is the best for great catches, you know, and they tend to follow us because the lights on their boats along with our lights are perfect bait for tarpon, speckled trout, grouper, snapper, and the like."

"Associated with the coast guard?" Rachel asked.

"No, but we see many of these old-timers when we are ashore, and we've gotten to know many of them. Good men! Most of them own their own boats. Quite a few of their vessels are decrepit, almost ready for the scrap heap. But see there," the captain said pointing to the area from which they came. "They are making good use of the searchlights we had on when we were in that area. It looks like they are taking in quite a haul. They don't bother us, you know."

The documents and licenses were returned. Martha

started up the engine again after the officers returned to their patrol boat. She steered it, making sure she didn't exceed the speed limit of 20 mph, and the coast guard boat followed right behind. She cautiously slowed the boat as they approached the dock, skillfully pulled alongside it, prepared the dock lines, and secured the boat before turning off the engine.

Up the hill, the lights were still on in Dr. Peltz's house, but Hunter's log cabin in the nearby woods was now dark.

"Lady, you sure do know how to handle this boat," the captain of the now idle patrol boat shouted. "I gotta hand it to you. Is that big house up there the doctor's home?"

"It sure is," Martha replied.

"I thought you said he was away for the weekend! Why are the lights on?"

"Oh, he always keeps some of them on while he is away. Always worried about burglars and all."

The coast guardsmen tipped their hats to the women and sped off back toward where they had spotted Martha's boat to rejoin the fishing boat, as the fishermen seemed to be struggling to bring in their heavy haul.

Martha and Rachel spent the rest of the night in the living room of Dr. Peltz's house, trying to decompress from the past day's surreal events and trying to make sense of it all. They remained wide awake.

"So how did you do it?" Martha asked Rachel after a lengthy silence.

"I told you that I wanted to pull out some of those beautiful oleanders in the garden here, the ones you showed me when we first met at Peltz's Sunday brunch. Of course, I knew that these plants are poisonous, even if you just touch them.[37] Any part of the plant, not just the flower; even its roots can cause death if eaten."

"And you wanted to feed him with it? They are almost never swallowed by people, you know, because their taste is so bitter," said Martha. "They're really inedible."

"Precisely!" Rachel replied. "That's why the Passover seder was exactly the right setting to slip them into Peltz's servings of maror, herbs that are just as bitter, mixed in some servings as a salad. People during a Passover meal *expect* it to taste like that. In the kitchen, as you saw, I insisted on coaching you to prepare Peltz's dishes myself without touching the sacred ingredients and doing it separately at a different kitchen table. We put on those surgical gloves that I brought from the clinic, which the other ladies across the kitchen found peculiar. I then finely chopped up the oleander leaves and roots and mixed them into the maror. I also insisted on serving Dr. Peltz myself, so I brought the dishes to him, not wanting anyone else to inadvertently touch them or give them to someone else."

"And no one said anything," Martha remarked.

"Well, there was a bit of commotion in the kitchen, as you know. Some of the women later wondered why I was being so antisocial and reclusive. I told them that I was just adding some ingredients that I had been told Dr. Peltz particularly liked, and I wanted it to be a surprise. Some of the women became quite nosy in fact, and one of them, that busybody Mrs. Feldman, demanded to know if those ingredients I used were kosher certified!" Rachel replied.

Martha then brought up a question that had been bothering her for some time.

"We have come to despise Dr. Peltz, now that we know about his dark background. And we've found out that he is doing illegal experiments on some of his patients without their permission, giving them drugs that could even be fatal.

But Rachel, you really do seem to have taken a special interest in getting rid of him, maybe more than any of us."

"I suppose so," replied Rachel. "It's a long story that someday I will tell you."

With sunrise, the two women cleaned up the first floor of the house, disposed of any potentially incriminating evidence, turned out the lights, and left, locking the doors behind them. Martha drove back to Tallahassee in her own car and gave a ride to Rachel.

Rachel's husband knew about some of what had been planned concerning Dr. Peltz. How could he not? When Rachel came home from work later that day, David was already there. He appeared to be uncharacteristically nervous and wound up about the possible consequences of what he called that "criminal act" that had been carried out by Rachel and Martha. And he was annoyed that Rachel had to get herself involved in this matter in the first place. Rachel tried to reassure him that it *had* to be done—that it was the right thing to do. She felt strongly that this would be the end of the story, so she wasn't much worried.

"David, the one thing we have to do right now is to take Peltz's car to the airport and park it there," said Rachel. "We fabricated that his absence now is due to his travel to New York for a prolonged period to continue his medical research there."

They waited until dark, drove to the temple where David had parked Peltz's car, and took it to the parking lot of the new Tallahassee Municipal Airport, leaving its doors unlocked. Rachel drove them back.

28

Dr. Peltz Is Away

When Dr. Peltz failed to appear at the clinics on Monday and Tuesday, Dr. Stanton, his young partner, became concerned. Dr. Peltz repeatedly didn't answer his home phone. So after office hours, Dr. Stanton drove to his house in Apalachicola. Nobody appeared at the door after he rang the doorbell insistently, several times. The house was dark. He looked around the streets nearby and couldn't see Dr. Peltz's parked car anywhere. From back in his office, Dr. Stanton then called all the nearby hospitals to see if Dr. Peltz had been admitted to any of them for some reason in the last few days. None of them had a record of him being there. By Friday, with Dr. Peltz's continued absence, and with staff and patients becoming increasingly alarmed, he drove to the Wakulla County Sheriff's Office to file a missing person's report. The sheriff assured him that his office would immediately send a copy of the report to the Leon County Sheriff's Office in Tallahassee because in missing person cases like this they had to work together sometimes.

A search was promptly initiated in both counties. Martha

and Rachel provided any contact information they had for people in New York who might know his whereabouts there. No one had seen him or heard from him there either. Most disturbingly, Dr. Harold Abramson's office at Mount Sinai Hospital, with whom Peltz had said he worked on the covert, CIA-sponsored brain research, indicated that Dr. Abramson hadn't been seen or heard from him in many years!

Two pairs of FBI agents from Washington were assigned to the case, and two detectives were appointed by the sheriff's offices of Leon and Wakulla counties, from their respective Criminal Investigations Divisions. At first, these pairs of federal and local agents worked separately, and only later did they begin to share information with each other, as directed by their superiors at the FBI and the sheriffs' offices.

Two breakthroughs occurred in short order. First Dr. Peltz's unlocked car was found in the Tallahassee airport's parking lot, with nothing inside it that might suggest where he was going. Second, a recorded message was found on Dr. Peltz's office telephone in Panacea.[38] It was from an FBI agent named Paul Adams, who wanted to schedule an urgent follow-up visit to Panacea to ask Dr. Peltz further questions concerning his illicit distribution of certain medications to some of his patients. No sooner than the message was picked up by the staff, agent Adams and another FBI colleague appeared in person at the Colored Only clinic. They showed their identifications. They were told that Dr. Peltz hadn't been seen or heard from for almost two weeks now. They believed he must be on a prolonged visit to New York.

"When was the last time anyone saw him?" FBI agent Adams asked Dr. Stenton.

"We saw him on Friday morning, April 8," he replied.

"Did he appear all right?"

"Very much so. Later in the day he left early for Passover

seder in Tallahassee. One of his patients who was there told us the next morning that he got sick at the dinner. GI stuff, you know. Apparently at his insistence, he was driven back to his Apalachicola home by some friends."

"So he may not have been able to come to his office for quite a while after that if he was that sick," the other agent said.

"I don't think so," Dr. Stanton replied. "First of all, no one answered the door of his home when I rang the bell the following day. And then there is a physician I met shortly after I arrived to practice in this area, a very nice obstetrician-gynecologist in Tallahassee, who was at the seder and drove him home. She said she stayed with him for a while. She told me afterward that Dr. Peltz just had simple gastroenteritis, and his symptoms were all mostly resolved by the next morning when they left."

"Her name …"

"Dr. Rachel Moran. She practices in Tallahassee. I have her phone number right here," Dr. Stanton said, flipping through his Rolodex.

The FBI agents then went to meet separately with the sheriffs of both Wakulla and Leon counties to compare notes and share the information they had regarding Dr. Peltz. The sheriffs had not known anything about the FBI's investigation into Dr. Peltz illicitly distributing experimental drugs to some of his patients without their knowledge and permission. They also didn't know that his Florida state medical license had been suspended recently for that reason. The sheriffs were taken aback by this shocking new information as they too had heard over years of the physician's pristine reputation in the community. The sheriffs promptly informed their detectives. From the FBI perspective, the issue of Dr. Peltz's disappearance was now a practically open-and-shut case. He simply fled from Florida, they figured, to avoid prosecution and, at the very least, permanent loss of his medical license to practice here. The agents had already interrogated the passenger manifests of all the airlines that had flights from Tallahassee since April 8. They even checked under what they by now knew was his real name, Hans Wilhelm König, again drawing a blank. As he had left his car at the airport, they reasoned that someone else or some others had facilitated his escape via other routes. The only alternative explanation was that his car at the airport was a ruse to distract from a very different form of disappearance.

The sheriffs, however, thought it was more likely that Dr. Peltz committed suicide, perhaps in response to the FBI's investigation into his dark background. Or maybe there was foul play. The Ku Klux Klan had harassed him several times in the past, so they should be considered suspects. In any case, it became clear that the FBI and the local sheriffs' offices would be best served by collaborating with each other from here on, one being a potential federal case and the other a state matter.

The Wakulla County detectives started their work by searching Dr. Peltz's two clinics and then his home, including its surroundings. The clinic searches didn't yield anything of importance that would be helpful. The personal files on the doctor's desk were in some disarray. They found receipts for flights and expenses related to his New York trips, architectural drafts for his new home and the clinics, miscellaneous correspondence of a personal nature, invoices from the Bluebird Apothecary in Frederick, Maryland, and financial reports from the Macy Foundation. They didn't know what to make of the last two items, so copies of all these papers were sent to their contacts at the FBI. Their search of his home likewise didn't uncover any useful information that could shed light on his disappearance.

They did find a scrap of folded paper on the living room floor that had the name Lieutenant Herbert Krüger, US Coast Guard, Panama City, on it. Probably nothing, they thought.

The Leon County detectives followed up with a further search of Dr. Peltz's abandoned car. They fingerprinted the steering wheel as well as the driver and passenger seats. They matched those of Peltz and those of Rachel Moran. The latter wasn't surprising as they already knew that Rachel had driven him home in his own car after the seder.

When the local authorities notified the FBI investigators about their unfruitful searches, they were told the FBI would send agents to also do searches, implying that the local efforts were not thorough enough.

A week later, two agents from the FBI, ones who had not been involved previously, arrived to search Dr. Peltz's home. As they knew that Martha had lived there for a while, they asked her to accompany them. Inspecting the inside of the house, they quickly found Dr. Peltz's locked office safe. They promptly engaged the services of another locksmith who had a more difficult time forcing it open. He drilled a hole on the side of the safe to unlock it from the inside. They took all the files to make copies of them, sent one set to the bureau's headquarters in Washington and perused another set to see if there were any incriminating pieces of evidence related to his disappearance or to the illicit drug trials he had conducted on his patients.

Nothing obvious was found inside the house, so they asked Martha to show them around the outside. Martha was quite proud of the gardens that she had herself helped to plant. One of the agents spotted an area that appeared to have been dug up. They walked over to look at where a bed of flowers probably had been planted.

"What was here?" one of them asked Martha.

"Oh, those were some beautiful oleanders. There are still some here," she said pointing to them. "See?"

"Do you know what happened to the others?"

Martha hesitated and fell silent. "I really don't know," she stuttered, putting her hand to her mouth. "My goodness, I just don't know ... maybe some roaming animal, like a dog or some other creature, chewed them up ... they look so attractive even to animals, you know."

The FBI agents made a note of it and then thanked Martha for her help.

They now focused their investigation on the individuals who had last seen Dr. Peltz. Foremost in their minds was Dr. Rachel Moran. They arranged for a full hour to interview her. It took place in her doctor's office after working hours.

29

The Interviews

The two FBI agents arrived on time, rang themselves in to enter the office, and appeared at Rachel's open door, knocking on it.

One was tall and quite youthful looking, wearing a felt fedora hat, indented on top, and the brim angled up in the back and down in the front. He had on chunky eyeglasses. The short man was older, overweight with a prominent waist, in a rumpled gray suit, wearing a white shirt with a drab-colored tie. The tall agent tipped the brim of his hat farther down before taking it off.

They introduced themselves. The tall agent's name was Michael Scarpano, and the short one's was Steve Whiteside. They sat down in chairs across from Rachel's office desk, facing her. Scarpano put his briefcase on Rachel's desk and asked her for permission to tape the conversation. Rachel was a bit taken aback but agreed to it. It was a clunky briefcase tape recorder, which Whiteside now turned on. Without any introductory chitchat, the agents got down to business.

"Dr. Moran, thank you for being so generous with your

time," began Scarpano. "I must say you have a splendid reputation in this community."

No response.

"Tell us briefly about your background."

Rachel didn't know how much detail they wanted, so she began hesitantly.

"I was born and raised by Jewish parents in the city of Szeged in Hungary. My father worked in food processing, including the city's famous paprika. Until the war, we lived a pleasant, uneventful life. But as the Nazi deportations came, my large family was widely dispersed to concentration camps, forced labor camps, and the like. Quite a few just disappeared, never to return to Szeged again."

Both agents were shaking their heads sympathetically, as if they had never heard of the Holocaust.

"Somehow, I survived," Rachel continued. "The circumstances were just too painful for me to retell. I hope you will understand."

The agents were taking notes even as the tape recorder was running, so they didn't look up at Rachel at all.

"After the war, I was admitted to the medical school in Budapest. Something that would have been impossible for a Jew to do before the war, you know. Then I came alone to America to do a residency in gynecology at the University of Florida. That's where I met my future husband, who was finishing his PhD there. David then got a faculty appointment at FSU, up here in Tallahassee, and I came with him to be on the staff of TMH."

"TMH?"

"Tallahassee Memorial Hospital. Another gynecologist was much needed in the area, so I was warmly welcomed. And this is where we planted our roots to raise children."

"So, Dr. Moran, how did you get to know Dr. Hans Wilhelm König, alias Dr. Ernest Peltz?"

"Well, when he moved to this area, he was keen on getting to know the medical community here. And he really did develop a very good word-of-mouth reputation as a hard-working and decent doctor. He joined the staff of the hospital and even came to some of the physician staff meetings. So we all got to know him."

"Before the night of his disappearance, had you ever been in his home?"

"Yes, once. He was living at that time along with his housekeeper, Martha Langston. There were some nasty rumors at that time, but it was strictly a professional relationship. Have you met her?"

"Not yet."

"Well, with Martha's help, Dr. Peltz hosted some Sunday brunches at his home and invited interesting people in the community. By then, he knew my name and my husband David's, and we were invited one time, along with some other FSU faculty members."

"Do you remember, Dr. Moran, any unusual moments that day you were in his house?"

"Unusual moments? Hmm," replied Rachel, closing her eyes and touching her lower lip with her index finger, trying to remember anything unusual. "No, not really; you know, it was just a pleasant afternoon."

"Any other time—"

"Wait a second," Rachel interrupted. "Now that you mention it, there *was* a point when my husband, David, Dr. Peltz, and an FSU art professor got into a heated exchange about a painting on the living room wall. It was a very small piece of art and showed some dancers."

"So do you remember what the argument was about?"

"Well, Dr. Peltz had a very nice art collection, and this one was by a famous painter, ... what's his name ... Dela? ... no, it was Degas."

"And what was the dispute?"

"It had something to do with where Dr. Peltz got the painting."

"And?"

"He said he bought it in New York, I think."

"And what was the dispute about?"

"It had something to do with the fact that the painting had been owned earlier by a wealthy Jewish family in Hungary, looted by the Nazis during the war, and now thought to have disappeared."

"Were there any other social events where you and Dr. Peltz were together?"

"Yes, I remember only one other, which I had to leave early when I started to not feel well. We were invited to the home of Mrs. Ilona Dohnány, whose husband had recently died. He was a very famous classical composer and pianist. Come to think of it, his first name was also Ernst. Just like Dr. Peltz, who was also there. It was a lovely afternoon with tea and the music of the Maestro played on a record player. But I remember repeatedly looking at Dr. Peltz, who seemed eerily familiar to me from the past. I was racking my brain so hard to place him and then began to feel extremely ill. David had to take me home. I was so embarrassed."

The agents paused, turned the pages of the notebooks on which they were taking notes, and continued.

"So, Dr. Moran, let's move on to your involvement in the events of the evening Dr. Peltz was last seen."

"Well, he became acutely ill at the seder with severe gastrointestinal symptoms that were almost disabling in severity. I and others at the dinner tried our best to convince him to allow us to call an ambulance to take him to the hospital, but he stubbornly and repeatedly refused. Said he just wanted to be taken home so that he could get over the illness there. So Martha and I drove him to his house in Apalachicola. We watched him through the night. He seemed to be getting worse at first but insisted that we leave him alone. We couldn't do that, so we sat in his living room, taking turns to look in on him in his bed in the ground floor bedroom. He did seem to be better. From the living room through a closed door, we even overheard him talking with someone on the phone.

As a physician, I knew that food poisoning or whatever else he had, a gastroenteritis of some kind, would be self-limited."

"One last question, Dr. Moran. Did you and your friend Martha go out in Dr. Peltz's motorboat that night?"

"Yes, we did. After he told us we must leave, and there was not much else we could do for him, we decided to unwind by taking a quiet boat ride out into the Gulf."

The FBI agents closed the meeting with Rachel and politely thanked her for her cooperation, indicating that they might have other questions later.

Next, Scarpano and Whiteside called Martha for an interview at her house. They didn't say anything about their meeting with Rachel.

"Mrs. Langston, tell us about how you got to meet Dr. Peltz," Scarpano started.

"Long story," replied Martha. "I've lived in this part of Florida all my life. I had the misfortune of marrying an abusive, alcoholic husband, a bigoted man who forced me to go with him to his Klan rallies."

"Klan?"

"Ku Klux Klan. White cloaks, burning crosses, speeches that spewed hatred. The whole business. We lived in a f****ng trailer in the forest. My relationship with Otis ... that's my husband's name ... came to a head one stormy night when he beat me up so badly that I lost consciousness. He was reeking of alcohol and stale cigarette smoke and held a kitchen knife to my throat. He threatened to take away my son by him, Jimmy, who was living with my sister Louisa in Tallahassee for safekeeping. He said he would kill the boy and cut out his heart. Dr. Peltz was our physician—we both had liver problems—and I trusted and liked him very much for the brief time we knew him, so I picked up Jimmy from Louisa's house in the storm and brought him with me to Dr. Peltz's home. We knew where he lived because my stepson, Hunter, was his housekeeper."

"Where did this boy Hunter live?" Whiteside asked.

"Very close to Dr. Peltz, in a log cabin the doctor had built for him on the edge of the forest," Martha replied.

"So you showed up that night at Dr. Peltz's door, in the storm and unannounced?"

"Yes. I just didn't know where else to go for safety. Dr. Peltz was so kind at that time that he not only took us in on the spot, but he also gave me a part of his beautiful, big house to settle into. Later, he helped me separate myself from the miserable environment I had been barely tolerating."

"And what was your relationship with him?"

"Not at all romantic or personal, if that's what you mean. All business."

"What kind of business?"

"At first, I helped Hunter with the housekeeping. Then the doctor hired me to work in his medical offices in Panacea. Later, he promoted me to help oversee his expanding practices when he realized that I wasn't quite as dumb as I looked and spoke. I was what people hereabouts called *trailer trash*, that's all."

"And so that was the relationship you continued to have with him right up to the time of his disappearance?" Whiteside asked.

"Oh God, no. I became disillusioned when I discovered that he was passing out experimental drugs to certain patients without even telling them what they were for, much less getting their permission. Then, as his mood became darker and darker, he ordered me to monitor their medical conditions after starting those drugs. I had to keep a logbook."

"Do you have that logbook, Mrs. Langston?"

"I don't. The FBI has taken over that part of the investigation."

"Yes, we know, and we don't want to interfere with those proceedings. But where did you go to expose this problem with experimental drugs?"

"By then I had befriended Dr. Rachel Moran, up in Tallahassee, who sorta took me under her wings to pretty much make me what I am today. After some of the patients receiving those drugs died or disappeared, she reported the matter to the Florida State Medical Association, which then took prompt action."

"Finally, Mrs. Langston, tell us about the night you last saw Dr. Peltz," Scarpano said.

"Rachel … Dr. Moran … invited me to the Passover dinner at the temple. I am a Christian, of course, and I was so pleasantly surprised by how hospitably I was received by the congregation. Dr. Peltz was there, and he became suddenly sick during the dinner. He told Rachel and others around him that he refused to go to the hospital. So Rachel drove him back to his home and wanted me to come along and help."

"What happened then?"

"Well, the two of us looked after him through the night ... until he started to get better."

"Was there anyone else there?"

"Rachel's husband, David, who drove his car behind us that night, just helped us carry Dr. Peltz into the house. Then it was just Rachel and me ... no, wait, my stepson, Hunter, came by since he was still his caretaker, living in a log cabin nearby so that he could always keep an eye on the house. He had seen the lights turned on, I suppose, and he wanted to know what was going on."

"Did he get involved?"

"Not really," Martha replied. "He looked in on him. And then he came out appearing distracted."

"Mrs. Langston, what do you think really happened to Dr. Peltz?" Whiteside probed.

Martha paused to think.

"Mrs. Langston?"

"I really don't know. I guess he either escaped, or he is dead. You gentlemen are the experts on this."

"Do you still hold bad feelings for him?"

"Yeah. How can I not, now knowing that he experimented on the patients who trusted him so much, a few of whom died or disappeared as a result. He also lied about his background and his Jewish religion. My friend Rachel shares my feeling, maybe even more so than me."

"Thank you, Ms. Langston, you've been most helpful."

As the two men started to leave and were out the door, Whiteside stopped, hesitated, and then turned back with an unexpectedly kind smile. "Ms. Langston," he said, "I can't help saying this, but who in God's name would ever call you trailer trash?"

"Well, I *was*," Martha replied.

Scarpano now turned halfway around and tipped his hat. "No, ma'am. You *never were!*"

The tape recordings of the FBI interviews with Rachel and Martha were securely shared with the sheriffs of both counties and their respective Criminal Investigations Divisions. The reciprocal understanding was that interviews conducted by the sheriff's offices of Wakulla and Leon Counties would also be securely shared with the FBI. The same applies to other investigative activities like searches, documents recovered, and inquires.

This was a complex case because Dr. Peltz's fraud and misconduct concerning his illicit use of experimental drugs that were illegally transported across state lines was potentially a federal crime, under the purview of the FBI, while the missing person or foul play issues were state and county matters that were within the scope of the county sheriffs. But as matters evolved, it became obvious that they couldn't be clearly separated. They overlapped and required this kind of synergistic cooperation between the agencies to expedite the case.

Two Wakulla County detectives went to interview Hunter Langston, Martha's stepson and ostensible caretaker of Dr. Peltz's estate. He was often difficult to understand, so the meeting was taped with Hunter's permission.

"Tell us, Hunter, about your relationship with Dr. Peltz."

"Ah've had thus job ever since thuh doctor arrived here, and Ah ain't regretted it wun bit, you know," Hunter replied.

"How so?"

"Hay has always treated may wayul and supported me with uh nice salary, you know."

"How much did he pay you?"

"Ahm not supposed tuh say it, but Ah git bout one hundred dollars uh week."

"That's very nice, Hunter. Has the doctor ever told you what he would do with his property and money if he died?"

"Oh yayus, he once sayud A'hd gut it all."

"That would be awfully generous," said one of the detectives as they both restrained their chuckles.

"So now, did Dr. Peltz ever tell you that his life was in danger, or did you ever see or hear anything that would indicate that?"

"Thet's confusin'. Whut wuz thuh fursd wun, sir, can you repeat it?"

"Life in danger?"

"Hay nevur railly sayud thet as far as Ah can remember. But hay often sayud hay wuz afraid."

"Afraid of what?"

"Thuh Klan ... Martha sumtimes ... sum uh thuh doctors and sum uh thuh Jews up in Tallahassee, you know."

"And did you ever see or hear anything that was suspicious?"

"Ah can't remember raht now ... but hey, wait uh minute there ... just uh few weeks ago, ah heard sum noise comin' frum ovur there."

"His house?"

"Yes. And Ah came upon a woman in thuh middle uh thuh night, diggin' up sum flowers in thuh doctor's garden. Whut thuh hell, Ah thought tuh me."

"Who was she?"

"When Uh turned on my flashlight and asked who she wuz, it that doctor woman from Tallahassee, Dr. Moran. Rachel. Thuh wun Dr. Peltz sayud hay wuz most frayed of."

"Can you come and show us where they were doing this?

Hunter led the two detectives to Dr. Peltz's house and to the spot in the garden that had been dug up.

A shrub remained in the dug-up garden plot, and from it a few flowers still blossomed with pink petals with long narrow leaves.

One of the detectives bent down and started to pluck one when Hunter suddenly grabbed his arm and loudly said:

"Don't touch them! Thay is very poisonous, them oleanders!"

"Damn!" the detective shot back as he immediately sprung up on his feet.

"So one more thing, Hunter. Your stepmother, Martha, told our detectives that the night Dr. Peltz got sick and disappeared, you came over to his house to look in on him."

"Yayus, sir, hay wuz very sick."

"Did he say anything to you?

"Hay sayud hay wuz in trouble and asked me tuh call uh friend uh his from the coast guard who could help him go to a hospital in Pensacola. He didn't want to go to the hospital up in Tallahassee."

"And then what happened?"

"Well, ... then hay gave me uh piece uh paper with his name an' contact information on it."

"Do you have it?"

"Naw, Ah guess Ah lost it somewhere."

"What happened after that?"

"Ah went back to mah house cuz Ah had friends over," replied Hunter.

"Did you see anything else happen that night?"

"Round 'bout two o'clock, Ah suppose, way wuz havin' sum beers outside on thuh grass overlookin' thuh water ... already quite drunk by then, Ah must say. Ah saw two paypul walkin' down to thuh dock ..."

"Did you recognize them?"

"Naw, sir. It wuz pitch dark an' thuh moonlight didn't help much."

"Could they have been your stepmother, Martha, and that Dr. Rachel Moran?"

"Wayul, Ah suppose so, Ah guess. Martha *did* say thet night that thay would go out on thuh fishin' boat fahwar uh while. Thay wuz carryin' uh big bag between them. Refreshments and towels, Ah thought."

"Thank you, Hunter," one of the detectives said, "you were very helpful."

While the interviews were proceeding, Mrs. Feldman appeared unannounced at the Leon County Sheriff's Office and excitedly told the receptionist that she needed to talk to the sheriff right away to give him information about the disappearance of Dr. Peltz.

The receptionist looked her over, up and down, sighed deeply, and slowly stood up to go into the office, shaking her head.

A deputy sheriff came out and asked Mrs. Feldman to follow him into one of the interview rooms.

"You are not the sheriff, young man," she protested gruffly, stopping in her track. "I want to see the real sheriff. What I have to say is too important."

"Sorry, Ma'am, but he is at court today," said the deputy.

"Well then," Mrs. Feldman said, "I'll just wait here until he gets back."

"I wouldn't advise that, Ma'am. He may be there all day and even all day tomorrow," replied the deputy, mustering all the tact he could without telling her off. However, Mrs. Feldman was implacable and sat back down in the waiting area in a huff, crossing her arms over her chest in a theatrical gesture of protest.

"Well, if it's that important and urgent, let me take some notes from you, and I'll be sure to share them with the sheriff as soon as he is available."

Mrs. Feldman had no choice but to capitulate, so she stood up and followed the deputy, stomping and muttering something incoherent to herself all the way into the interview room.

"So, Mrs. Feldman, please tell me what you know," the deputy started from his seat, with a pad of paper in front of him on the desk and a pen in hand. "You should first know that we are formally interviewing a lot of people who might know something about the circumstances of this case."

"Well then," Mrs. Feldman countered, "you now have this volunteer, little old me, who knows more than any of the others. I have much reason to believe that Dr. Peltz was murdered! And I know who did it!"

She was waiting for a shocked response from the deputy, but he calmly just said, "Go on!"

"Dr. Peltz was a much-beloved and highly respected member of the Jewish community in Tallahassee, you should know that. And he was a marvelous doctor, I can testify. My husband and I have been his patients. But there were a few who *did* hate him. Dr. Calhoun and his doctor colleagues, for one, because they were envious of his success or because they were anti-Semitic. Dr. Rachel Moran, who you must have interviewed by now, …"

The deputy nodded.

"… another Jewish doctor here. She held some kind of personal grudge against Dr. Peltz that was obvious to many others in the Jewish congregation."

"What kind of grudge?" the deputy asked.

"I have *no* idea whatsoever, nor do the others."

"So tell me, Mrs. Feldman, if you think she was the murderer, how did she do it?"

"Young man, I think I know!" Mrs. Feldman replied. "She poisoned him. I saw it myself. I was working with other ladies in the kitchen during the seder, preparing the dishes we would serve, and that woman Moran was doing likewise. But she was alone, by herself, with a *goy* woman I had never seen before. They were working at a separate table, whispering to each other and acting very secretive and suspicious while they were also making dishes. I even sent my daughter over to their table to eavesdrop, and she confirmed that they were chatting about Dr. Peltz. I then saw Rachel Moran serving the dishes to Dr. Peltz herself. She insisted, she told some of the ladies. Now wouldn't you think that was suspicious?"

Before the deputy sheriff could respond, there was a knock on the door, and the receptionist stuck her head inside to ask the deputy to come out for a minute. When he returned, he expressed his apologies to Mrs. Feldman, stating that he was being called away for a very urgent matter.

"But what about me?" Mrs. Feldman asked indignantly.

"We'll have to take it up again another time, but I must go now," and with that he left, closing the door behind him, still hearing Mrs. Feldman yelling something about having no respect for her.

30

Bert

Scarpano, Whitehead, and one of the detectives who had just interviewed Hunter next made an appointment to talk with Lieutenant Herbert Krüger at the Coast Guard base in Panama City. They decided that all three should go because they had a hunch that this interview would be pivotal in the case.

The detectives arrived at the coast guard station on a hot afternoon in June 1963. Bert, dressed in uniform, greeted them at the entrance and escorted them inside after showing identification and getting "VISITOR" passes to stick on their shirts.

They sat in an over-air-conditioned small conference room with no windows and with institutional fluorescent lighting. Bert told a seaman recruit to bring cold drinks for everyone. Introductions were made.

"Lieutenant Krüger," started Scarpano, "I think you know that we are investigating the disappearance of Dr. Peltz, who I understand has been your physician and is a friend of your father. Do you know how they became friends?"

"Not exactly. They graduated from the same university in Germany. But my father is not a physician; he is a mathematician."

"All right," said Whiteside, "you probably also know that on the night before his disappearance in April, Dr. Peltz became extremely ill during a Passover seder in Tallahassee, and he was driven to his home instead of to a hospital, allegedly at his own insistence. There, Martha Langston, who knew the doctor well, along with another woman he may have also known, Dr. Rachel Moran. The two women together drove him to his home in Apalachicola and then tended to him there overnight."

"Yes, I know that. But I wouldn't say Dr. Peltz was *extremely* ill," Bert said.

"Hmmm. How would you know that, Lieutenant?" Scarpano asked in a distrusting tone.

"Because I spoke with him on the phone that night, after he had been taken back to his home. We talked very briefly, and he said he was much better."

"Was he coherent?"

"Yes, he was. But he was whispering into the phone. He spoke quite intelligibly, but he was expressing some paranoid thoughts."

"What was your reaction to those thoughts, Lieutenant?"

"Well, I know from my father that ever since they first met, Dr. Peltz repeatedly told him about a plot to kill him. He was sure it was going to be by drowning. Funny he should say that. He was a champion long-distance swimmer back in Germany, you know. I think he swam for Germany in the 1936 Olympics in Berlin. Ironic. My father at first just shrugged off these comments as flights of the imagination. Not completely surprising for a Jewish man living in Nazi Germany, you know. But later, his paranoid thoughts became more frequent and disturbing.

So Dr. Peltz called me that night and said he was poisoned and was going to be drowned shortly in the Gulf. He wanted me to send a coast guard boat out to the area close to his home, just for surveillance."

Bert stood up and left for a minute, returning with some objects inside a plastic bag on a tray. Bert and the detectives put on white gloves that were supplied so that they could inspect the objects.

"The two women in the fishing motorboat matter-of-factly identified themselves as Martha Langston and Rachel Moran when my officers boarded it. These are what my officers found in the fishing motorboat that night. This one here," Bert said, passing it around, "is a bracelet that's engraved on the inside. We think it belongs to Rachel Moran."

"Yes, it is," said Whitehead, "When we interviewed her, Dr. Moran confirmed that she lost it in the boat and couldn't find it in the dark."

The detectives could make out only some of the engraving on the inside of the ring with a magnifying glass: "Dr. Levi Ráhelm," and "1948."

"Ráhelm was Dr. Moran's given Jewish name," said Whitehead, who had been informed by Rachel, "and 1948 was the year she graduated from medical school. So it must have been a graduation present."

It was carefully placed back into its plastic bag.

"Now this one," said Bert, passing around a large, blackened coin, about two inches in diameter, "looks like a brass medal that has become badly oxidized. We had no idea who this belonged to, but some suspected it might have belonged to Dr. Peltz. The only snag with that, but an important one, was that we were told that Dr. Peltz never used the boat himself. One of our staff tried to rub off the black stain with a salt-vinegar paste. So here we can see on one side what looks like a *hoheitszeichen*, the notorious eagle with a swastika, Nazi Germany's national emblem." Bert pointed to it with a sharpened pencil tip, barely touching it.

He then turned over the coin, the other side being still mostly blackened. Leaning into it with a magnifying glass, he pointed his pencil to some writing that could be barely made out. He passed it around and asked the others what they thought.

Whitehead was the first to speak up, haltingly identifying the letters: "K-Ö-N-I-G."

"What does that mean?" Scarpano asked.

"I think it means 'king,' but it's also a common German surname," replied Bert. "We will have to get a professional numismatist to clean up this medal or coin or whatever it is. That's what I was told."

"So do you think it belonged to Dr. Peltz?" the detectives asked Bert.

"No," Bert replied, "I don't think so. My father told me one time that Dr. Peltz never used the fishing boat himself, hated boats. So he allowed his guests to use it."

31

Indictment

The Second Judicial Circuit of Florida encompassed the state's panhandle, including Leon and Wakulla counties. The state attorney of the Second Circuit was the chief prosecutor, primarily focused on criminal offenses. In November 1963, the chief prosecutor of the Second Judicial District decided that sufficient evidence had been accumulated in this case to convene a grand jury in Wakulla County to consider the indictment of Rachel for the murder of Dr. Peltz and Martha for being an accomplice to that murder. After several weeks of hearing the evidence against the defendants by the prosecutor and deliberating, the grand jury found the evidence to be sufficient for the indictment of Rachel and of Martha as an accomplice to the crime. The indictments were filed with the county court. The trials would be separate, of course.

Florida State University was planning to open a law school at that time. So prospective faculty members became excellent sources for recommending a couple of well-known defense attorneys for the two women. The lawyers accompanied them to the women's arraignment where Rachel and Martha were separately read the charges against them. Having had an opportunity to review the details of the case against them, the attorneys recommended to both women a plea of "not guilty." Rather than a bench trial, the defense asked for a jury trial.

At the arraignment, the judge considered the conditions of releasing the women on personal recognizance. Despite the seriousness of the indictments, both Rachel and Martha were felt to have strong community roots with solid jobs and no personal criminal records, so the judge waived bail.

It was very unusual to pursue a criminal murder trial without a *corpus delicti*, in the absence of the corpse of the murder victim. But the law was that a defendant could be charged and even convicted of murder *without* a corpse if enough circumstantial evidence existed for a jury to conclude that the victim is in fact dead and that the defendant is guilty. Just a couple of years earlier, the California case of People v. Scott had held that "circumstantial evidence, when sufficient to exclude every other reasonable hypothesis, may prove the death of the missing person, the existence of a homicide, and the guilt of the accused."[39]

32

Alligator Point

Rachel's trial was set to begin on April 1, 1964. But by jarring coincidence a body was found washed ashore on the sandy beach of Alligator Point. The corpse was quite badly decomposed. Florida didn't have a regional network of medical examiners. So to prevent much more putrefaction of the body, it had to be promptly driven to the morgue of Tallahassee Memorial Hospital in a truck equipped with a Cool Pack AC unit. The physician who did the autopsy was a pathologist named Dr. Stewart Bradshaw. However, Dr. Bradshaw had no experience or formal training in forensics. By the time the autopsy was completed, word had spread rapidly around the Florida panhandle about the young boy who found the washed-up corpse on the beach at Alligator Point while fishing with his father, even before the newspapers or TV had a chance to report it. And, along with the word of mouth, townspeople around Panacea and Apalachicola were already murmuring that the corpse was that of Dr. Peltz.

Dr. Bradshaw used whatever tools were available to identify the body. He was able to obtain Dr. Peltz's anthropometric data like height, weight, other body dimensions, eye and hair color from his driver's license, his Florida Board of Medicine state registration, and his passport, all of which became available to investigators after his disappearance. Using these identifiers, Dr. Bradshaw concluded that the measurements of the corpse were completely consistent with those measurements known about Dr. Peltz. He was able to aspirate some blood clot from the left ventricle of the corpse and send it for ABO typing. It matched the ABO type of Dr. Peltz from his files and medical records at Tallahassee Memorial Hospital. Not only did it match; it was one of the rarest types among Caucasians, B-negative. Otherwise, further information from the badly decomposed corpse was practically impossible to ascertain given the available technology. The corpse was grotesquely bloated and putrified; the skin was almost entirely sloughed, and what little remained of it was dramatically wrinkled, making fingerprinting impossible. Much of the body was covered by a yellow-brown waxy material composed of fatty acids, referred to in forensic medicine as adipocere formation. The body's surface condition would have made it nearly impossible to identify distinctive skin markings like moles, hemangiomas, or tattoos. What were found, however, were numerous scars, abrasions, deep cuts, and carved out areas of soft tissue and torn muscle. At first glance they would have suggested traumatic injuries that could have been inflicted before death. However, the same kinds of bodily damage could have been likewise caused by the dead body being dragged underwater for long distances and getting caught on rocks, branches, and other objects, as well as the gross tissue damage that would be inflicted by animal predation and microorganisms.[40] No dental records for Dr. Peltz were found in the region or in

New York. Dr. Bradshaw's report concluded that, especially given the facts surrounding Dr. Peltz's disappearance, the autopsy findings were very consistent with but "perhaps not completely conclusive" of the identity of Dr. Peltz. The prosecutors couldn't believe the serendipity of this finding two months before the start of the trial.

33

The Trial

The Wakulla County Courthouse (Second Circuit) was located on Crawfordville Highway. It was a nondescript, uninspiring, three-story white stucco building with a flat roof. It had four unadorned, flat columns built almost undistinguishably into the façade. Five large, slatted windows in a row were situated above the main entrance. It's a building one can easily drive by or even walk by without noticing it—nothing like the charming wooden courthouses of the Old South with their clock towers and steeples. The trial had been receiving much publicity within the larger community in the newspapers, on radio, and on TV news, and had been the subject of many conversations among citizens. After all, no one in these parts could remember a trial in which a physician was indicted on a charge of murder. So on the first day the spectator gallery was filled.

Rachel's husband David sat in the first row, just behind his wife, every day of the trial. Martha was not allowed in the courtroom to hear the testimonies because she would likely be indicted for aiding and abetting in the commission of the crime if Rachel was found guilty.

The courtroom was now abuzz with chatter, anticipating the arrival of the judge. Rachel sat at the defense counsel table with her back to the spectators, flanked by her two lawyers. She wore a conservative navy suit and same color pencil skirt below the knees. Under the suit, as always, she had a long-sleeved light blue shirt.

One of Rachel's two defense attorneys was the veteran litigator Holden Cunningham, a man in his late sixties who was well known and highly respected throughout the Deep South for his long and successful career as a defense attorney in criminal trials, with a track record of effectively representing some high-profile defendants in complex and controversial cases. He had an enormous depth of knowledge of criminal law, and his communication skills at trial were unsurpassed in the area, speaking slowly with a velvety Southern drawl, and calmly, with great clarity, in a sonorous voice that could become thunderous at well-chosen, strategic points in the trial. Cunningham's junior colleague was Chase Aiken, a *summa cum laude* Yale graduate, an editor of its *Law Review*, who had a few years earlier completed an investigative internship in criminal law at one of Atlanta's most prestigious firms. Aiken was now rapidly gaining recognition as an energetic, dedicated, and innovative criminal trial attorney who investigated the backgrounds of his clients' cases and prepared for their trials with amazing thoroughness. Importantly, Chase Aiken was born and raised by a poor family in Quincy, Florida, about forty miles north of Crawfordville, graduating from Quincy High School.

The court clerk was already in place to the right of the judge and next to the witness stand. The bailiff, Travis Dawson, dressed in a police officer's uniform, now appeared, stood still for a minute to let the clamor die down, and then announced, "This court will come to order!" The courtroom was immediately silenced. "All rise," and everyone rose, "with the Honorable Judge Graham Rutledge presiding, is now in session." Judge Rutledge, in his flowing black robe, walked in and up to the bench. "Please be seated," he said as he plopped into his leather chair.

Jury selection began from a pool of more than fifty citizens. Florida was one of the states where potential jurors who had a record of being merely charged with a misdemeanor offense in the past, even if they hadn't been convicted, were excluded. Although 30 percent of the population of Wakulla County was classified as "Negro," only one Black man was selected for jury service. This was because Rachel's lead defense attorney excluded ten other qualified Black jurors by "preemptory strike."[41] The judge allowed this number even though the defense had exceeded its limit of preemptory challenges, that is, challenges without stated cause that didn't require explanation. He felt that Dr. Peltz's very large and loyal patient practice of Blacks, as well as his fine reputation within their community, would bias Black jurors, who might harbor animosity toward his purported murderer. Two qualified Jewish men were also struck. Twelve jurors and three alternates were finally agreed upon by the two sides and the judge.

The lead prosecutor was an elected state attorney, as was required in Florida, who represented the Second Judicial Circuit Court, which included Wakulla County. He was a young South Carolinian man named Drew Griffin, who already had an established reputation for being a fast-talking, aggressive, and fierce interrogator whose brashness and arrogance was not infrequently rebuked by judges. For the first day, Griffin appeared with perfectly coiffed, lustrous blond hair and wore a tailored off-white suit from Ben Silver in Charleston, with a shiny white Oxford cotton shirt and a bright, burgundy-based silk tie. The defense attorneys wore less fashionable 1950s style suits and ties.

Judge Rutledge greeted the seated jurors. Then he turned to the defense counsel's table and addressed Rachel.

"Ms ... excuse me, *Doctor* Rachel Moran. As you know, you have been charged with the first-degree murder of Dr. Ernest Peltz, also known as Dr. Hans Wilhelm König, on April 8–9, of 1963, in Tallahassee and Apalachicola. Would you please stand and raise your right hand."

Rachel stood up, visibly nervous for the first time.

"How do you plead, 'guilty' or 'not guilty'?"

"Not guilty, your Honor." She heard her own voice quivering, so she sat back down as soon as she was instructed to do so.

"Mr. Griffin," the judge said, "you may now make your opening statement to the jury."

At this, Griffin virtually jumped from his chair and made a beeline to the jury box, instantly forming a well-rehearsed, forced smile on his face on his way there. He lavishly thanked the jurors for their unselfish and patriotic service to their community and expressed his confidence in each and every one's sense of fairness, justice, and wisdom.

"What we have here, ladies and gentlemen of the jury, is an indisputable, open-and-shut case of a premeditated, planned murder of one of this community's irreplaceable treasures, a brilliant and devoted doctor who was beloved by his patients. The murderer ..."

He stepped back to the defense counsel's table and pointed at Rachel.

"... also a doctor but not at all known around these parts, likely held a grudge against Dr. Peltz or had professional jealousy of him. After all, Dr. Peltz had become a celebrity of sorts with an ever-growing panel of adoring patients."

At this point, Griffin began to pace up and down with resolve in front of the jury box. As he spoke with heightened histrionics, his pacing stereotypically resembled a caged lion.

"Dr. Peltz has never . . . ever . . . turned a patient away. He even expanded his practice by building a separate clinic for Negro patients who he treated just as conscientiously as his White patients, even though many of them couldn't pay. Money seemed to be the lowest of priorities for this extraordinary physician. These characteristics were opposed to those of the defendant who had no reputation ... have any of you ever heard of her? ... with a much smaller practice of paying patients who she cultivated for that purpose.

"Even when this case was going to court with corpus delicti, a phrase we use in a murder trial where the victim's corpse has not been found, the grand jury before you decided that sufficient evidence existed to indict the defendant for murder. But *now*, ... *now* we have found it. Washed ashore just some forty miles from where Dr. Peltz resided. You will hear from the expert pathologist who performed the autopsy that concluded that the body was indeed that of Dr. Peltz."

Attorney Griffin then rambled on for another half an hour, speaking more and more loudly, and pacing back and forth in front of the jury with increasing ferment, until Judge Rutledge leaned forward over his desk.

"Mr. Griffin," he said, "I am afraid you are going to have to wrap up now."

"But you Honor—"

"You have already said what you were going to say, I believe."

With that, Griffin concluded by theatrically prevailing on the jury.

"Ladies and gentlemen, we will prove beyond any reasonable doubt that the defendant, Rachel Moran, is guilty as charged of murder in the first degree, an act that was premeditated, reckless, and evil!"

The last word reached a crescendo of intensity.

"Mr. Cunningham," the judge turned to the defense counsel's table, "are you ready for your opening statement?"

"Ah certainly am, your Honor."

With that, Cunningham rose from his chair in slow motion. He was a much larger man than what might be ascertained when he was sitting. Maybe six feet four or six feet five, somewhat paunchy, slightly stooped, not fat but heavyset. He lumbered over to the jury box. Then he stood there for a while, grasping with both hands the railing that separated him from the two rows of jurors, silently leaning closer to them as he made eye contact with each one, scanning them from left to right and then right to left. Finally he started, slowly, with his lyric, honey-coated, baritone voice.

"Ladies and gentlemen. Lest you become alarmed, I want to assure y'all that I will not be anywhere nearly as long-winded as my prosecution counsel friend, a very fine orator, I must admit," turning toward Griffin and momentarily pointing to him with his open hand.

He stopped, inflated his chest, and placed his hands into the pockets of his vest. Some of the jurors looked at each other in puzzlement, but then, one by one, let out a cautiously muffled chuckle. Judge Rutledge also flashed a half smile. "Y'all will hear from us a completely different version of the events of April 8 and 9," Cunningham continued, "... and y'all will hear an entirely different picture of the defendant, Doctor Rachel Moran. What y'all will hear are the facts and the truth, not speculation.

"In fact, Attorney Chase Aiken, my colleague over there at

the counsel defense table, I myself, and others who helped us prepare for the trial were shocked, ... just *shocked*, ... I mean *dadgum dumbfounded* when we heard the grand jury's decision to proceed with this trial. So *why* were we so shocked? Because the evidence y'all will hear is so circumstantial, so doggone flimsy, and so plain and simply untrue that it won't take you long in the jury room to find my client not guilty—if we ever even need to get to that point in the proceedings.

"*Never*," Cunningham thundered, "in my long career, representing litigants on both sides in well over five hundred, more like a thousand murder trials, have I seen *this* degree of weakness in evidence."

34

Parade of Witnesses

After a brief recess, Judge Rutledge called on attorney Griffin to call his first witness for the prosecution. Griffin wanted to first demonstrate to the jury the extraordinary benevolence and decency of Dr. Peltz by calling three of his former patients as examples, thereby cultivating sympathy for the victim.

The first witness was Mrs. Annalee Gibson, a widow in her seventies, who was still a spry woman. "Mrs. Gibson, tell us for how long you have known Dr. Peltz," Griffin began.

"Oh goodness, since about 1958 … or even longer. I think my deceased husband and I were among his very first patients in this area."

"Were you also personal friends with him?"

Mrs. Gibson appeared to recoil in uneasiness. "No. Never. I would never even think about socializing with a doctor, especially a famous one like him!"

"Can you tell us how he treated you and your husband medically? What was his practice style?"

"Amazingly conscientiously. From day one. Whenever I

came to the clinic in Panacea, he treated me like I was his only patient, like nobody else mattered at that moment. When I had an illness, he would prescribe the right medications for me to get well soon. And then he or his nurse would always call me at home to see how I was feeling. A couple of times when I was too sick to get out of bed, he came for home visits. Like an old-fashioned doctor, he brought his black doctor's bag that was full of all sorts of instruments."

"Mrs. Gibson, were there times when he wasn't available, when you were sick and couldn't get help?"

"Well, he often left for weekends. He said he was doing important medical research in New York. But he had coverage on those occasions. Two young doctors who were nothing like him—there was nobody like him."

"Did he ever tell you what he was researching in New York?"

"No. I never asked because I knew I wouldn't understand it, and I didn't want to pry."

"So, Mrs. Gibson, how would you rate Dr. Peltz overall?"

"He was by far and away the best doctor I have ever had."

For cross-examination, Chase Aiken, Cunningham's junior colleague, stood and approached the witness stand.

"Mrs. Gibson, my name is Chase Aiken, the junior attorney for the defense. Just a few questions, if I may."

"Go ahead, dear," Mrs. Gibson replied.

"Please accept my condolences for your husband's passing. Can you tell us when that happened, and what was the cause of death?"

"Oh, he was quite a bit older, you know, but he was relatively healthy. Just high blood pressure. He died about two years ago. It was quite a shock. Nobody could tell me the cause of death, including Dr. Peltz. He thought it was a heart attack. But for a few months leading up to it he was losing his mind quite quickly."

"What was Dr. Peltz's opinion about his mental deterioration?" Aiken asked.

"I think he said he had dementia."

"All right. When Dr. Peltz was prescribing medications for you, were there any occasions when he gave them to you with strict instructions on how to take them and *without* charge?"

"No ... well, yes, actually. Last year he gave me some of those free white pills that I am still taking," she replied.

"Did he tell you the indication? The reason for giving them to you?"

"No, sir, and it wasn't my place to ask. After all, he always knew what he was doing."

"Was there a label on the bottle or anything carved onto the pills themselves?" Aiken continued.

"Well, my husband was the one who took them regularity, as instructed. I myself, for the few I took, never got them in a bottle or a vial or anything like that. They were always given to me in small plastic bags every time he refilled them. And I didn't really look for any writing on the pills themselves. What difference would it make?"

"Mrs. Gibson, would you be able to provide the court one of those pills to examine?"

Griffin leapt to his feet. "Objection, your honor! What is this charade all about? It has nothing to do with this trial. Is the defense trying to obfuscate and derail witness testimonies."

"Mr. Aiken—"

"Your Honor," Aiken interrupted. "Every question we ask has a reason for asking it. The events involved in this case are complex, and we just want to clear a path for understanding them."

"I will decide shortly. In the meantime, Mr. Aiken, please proceed."

"Mrs. Gibson, do you have any of those pills we can look at?" Aiken resumed.

"Sure, young man. I always take some with me. May I look in my handbag?"

Travis, the bailiff, brought out the bag from safe keeping at the judge's instructions. The judge took it first and then asked Travis to give it to the witness in order for her to search for a pill.

While all this was happening, attorney Griffin was becoming increasingly agitated. Unable to sit still even while whispering to his junior partner, he finally stood up again as Mrs. Gibson was searching her bag, which appeared to be overstuffed with various items. She was removing them one by one and, shaking her head, placing them on the shelf inside of the witness box.

"Your Honor," Griffin started in, "you must make a decision regarding my objection. What is happening here is highly irregular. What possible reason is there to bring up this witness's medications?"

"I got one!" Mrs. Gibson cried out, holding up a white pill like a Bingo winner.

"First, Mr. Griffin," the judge started with a serious scowl, "I don't *'must do'* anything! Didn't you learn that in law school? The judge in a criminal trial cannot be coerced to do *anything*. Not to mention the utter lack of respect you have shown."

"I apologize, Your Honor, I should not have said that."

"Mr. Aiken," the judge turned to defense counsel, "I don't see the reason either."

"We hope to show you and the jury the reason shortly."

"*Hope*?!" Griffin exploded.

"All right, all right," the judge said in exasperation. "Mr.

Griffin, Mr. Aiken, and Mr. Cunningham, I want you all in my chambers right now. And I ask the bailiff to bring the pill into chambers also."

The stenographer followed them with her shorthand machine to record the conversation in the chambers.[41]

The outcome of the closed meeting was that defense counsel would promptly present the reasons why Mrs. Gibson's pills might be important for this trial specifically. And a sample pill would be taken securely for a quick analysis by a reputable pharmacist nearby.

After questioning the next witness, a middle-aged farmer named Emmett Jones, another grateful Peltz patient, Holden Cunningham took over the cross-examination. Mr. Jones had testified right along the line of the previous patient's testimony, praising Dr. Peltz's rigorous training in Germany, his extensive experience in practice, and his stellar reputation in the Florida panhandle.

"Mr. Jones," Cunningham began, "my colleague previously asked another patient whether or not she had received medications from Dr. Peltz *gratis*, without charge. So I ask you the same question."

"Oh God, I got so many medications … I lose track of them, you know …"

"Do you recall getting free medications?"

"I just can't remember."

"Mr. Jones, are you aware that Dr. Peltz lost his state of Florida medical license some time ago? That he was barred from practicing medicine in this state?" Cunningham moved in to as close as he could to the witness stand, facing the witness practically nose to nose.

"No, sir. Why was he barred?" Mr. Jones asked with astonishment.

"I am not in a position to disclose that. In general, crimes or misconduct can lead to that decision, like improper prescribing of drugs, insurance fraud, commission of felony, substance abuse by the doctor, convictions not reported, and others."

"F**ck, you mean I have been seeing a doctor who has been doing something like that?"

"I am afraid so," Cunningham said softly.

Griffin stood again. "Objection, your honor. Again, we are being taken on an irrelevant journey to nowhere."

Cunningham responded. "Your Honor, prosecution has called witnesses to establish Dr. Peltz's exclusively salutary character. We therefore should be given the opportunity to counter that with a *well documented* dark side of Dr. Peltz."

"Your Honor," Griffin continued, "this is information we have never had."

"Well, Mr. Griffin, loss of a state medical license is public information. It is within the public domain, mostly to protect potential patients from unqualified and unlicensed physicians. And if you didn't have that information, Mr. Griffin, perhaps you should have done a better job of researching the victim's past."

"Objection overruled. Proceed, Mr. Cunningham."

"Go ahead, Mr. Jones, and finish what you were saying," Cunningham said.

"Well, ... what more can I say? I'm almost speechless. Dr. Peltz is ... I beg your pardon, *was* ... such a wonderful German man of Jewish faith," concluded Mr. Jones.

"He was never even Jewish, you know. And he stayed in Germany throughout the war and worked for Nazi Germany," Cunningham said.

35

Getting Warmer

The revelation of Dr. Peltz's alleged "dark side" brought an audible gasp throughout the courtroom, and then more and more visitors began to talk with others seated next to them, amplifying the noise level, "until Judge Rutledge pounded his gavel repeatedly.

"Order! Order in court!" he shouted. "Any more outbursts like this, and I'll instruct the bailiff to escort out of the courtroom anyone who does not comply!"

With that, Holden Cunningham felt that this would be a good point to stop. He thanked Mr. Jones and excused him. A third witness who was scheduled to testify regarding Dr. Peltz's character was now excused by the prosecution. Nothing more would be gained from her testimony.

The prosecution then called Mrs. Irene Feldman to the witness stand. There was some buzzing between Rachel and her lawyers, putting their heads together, as Mrs. Feldman walked to the front of the room to get sworn in and take her seat. Most witnesses approach the witness stand with trepidation, but Mrs. Feldman walked with pomp.

"Mrs. Feldman," Griffin started, "please tell us your full name, your occupation, and background."

"My name is Mrs. Irene Feldman. I am the widow of Isaac Feldman, who died of cancer a few years ago, may his memory be a blessing. We were both Holocaust survivors. We came to this country and Tallahassee, thankfully, when Isaac was invited to teach Hebrew studies in what was then a planned Department of Religion at Florida State University. Isaac was known worldwide for his scholarship in Jewish culture. He wrote many books on the subject.

"Now, all I have left in my family is my daughter, Sarah. She is now in ninth grade at Leon High School. I have been an active member of Tallahassee's growing Jewish congregation."

"OK. So, Mrs. Feldman, tell us how long you have known Dr. Peltz and the defendant, Rachel Moran," Griffin said.

"I have known Dr. Peltz for many years. He was my doctor as well as Isaac's. A wonderful man, may his memory be a blessing. As for Rachel Moran, *paskudnik*![43] A bad person. For a start, she married a goy. And she comes to Shabbat services on Friday evenings only when she wants to recruit more women to be her patients."

Rachel now leaned into her attorneys to whisper her protest to the blatant lies Mrs. Feldman was spouting.

"So, Mrs. Feldman, now tell us exactly what you saw or heard at the seder on the evening of April eighth and through the night of April ninth."

"I and several other devout women in the community were in the kitchen adjoining the congregation room that belongs to Temple Israel, busily preparing the seder ritual dishes. We expected one hundred people, so we were working crazy hard. Then Rachel Moran struts into the kitchen, accompanied by a woman we had never seen. That strange woman, who I later found out was Martha Langston, appeared very uncomfortable. And in no way was she Jewish by her appearance and name. A Gentile, a goy, for sure."

"What happened then?" Griffin probed.

"They walked into the kitchen, right past our food preparation table, without so much as a greeting, and set up shop on a separate, unoccupied table at some distance. We found it strange ... disturbing actually ... that the two women were preparing only *one* of the several special dishes of food that are consumed during a seder feast. And then we found out it was a single serving just for Dr. Peltz, nobody else. They kept whispering to each other while preparing the dish. I told my daughter, Sarah, to walk over there in an innocent way and find out what they were chatting about."

"And what did Sarah report back to you?"

"She said they were talking, whispering about Dr. Peltz."

"What happened after that?"

"Well, you know the rest. Dr. Peltz became extremely ill quite suddenly. Vomiting, diarrhea in the toilet, and very bad stomach cramps. And this was after he finished the dish that Rachel Moran personally served him."

"So, Mrs. Feldman, from these events you concluded that Rachel Moran killed Dr. Peltz by feeding him poison?"

"Huh! So what else would anyone conclude?" Mrs. Feldman snapped back.

"For argument's sake, why couldn't it have been Martha, for example? Martha putting the poison in his dish?"

"That goy bitch didn't have a clue," retorted Mrs. Feldman. "She wasn't even supposed to be there that night. She showed up unannounced, without anyone giving her permission to be there, especially in the kitchen."

"Thank you, Mrs. Feldman," Griffin concluded. "No further questions."

At this point, Rachel had become so agitated that she

huddled with her attorneys again, not whispering this time. She suggested to them that they should ask for a brief recess so that Rachel could explain to the lawyers how insane this woman is.

After the recess, Chase Aiken was about to get out of his chair to cross-examine the witness, but Cunningham grabbed his arm. "Let me do this one," he said.

"Mrs. Feldman," he started, "I gather from your comments that you and Dr. Rachel Moran are not the best of friends."

Muted laughter arose from around the courtroom. The judge frowned.

"I do apologize," Cunningham continued, "but I thought just a pinch of levity would improve the atmosphere around here. Let me get some things straight about the events you described.

"You said Martha Langston wasn't permitted to be at the seder. Pre-trial, we deposed Rabbi David Eichorn of Temple Israel, who has the final word, isn't that right?"

"After God, yes."

"Well, we have on record from him that he explicitly gave Martha permission to be at the seder that evening, as well permission to work in the kitchen. Later on that evening, the rabbi even looked inside the kitchen to see everyone and thank them. Do you remember that, Mrs. Feldman?"

"Well, let me think ... now I do recall he poked his head in ... but I don't know anything about permission."

"All right then. You testified that the defendant, Rachel Moran, prepared only one dish and that she personally served it to Dr. Peltz, without doing so for others—"

"That's right," Mrs. Feldman interrupted.

"But we have several witness accounts by people at the

seder, who were also deposed, that the defendant was seen circulating around the large room and serving other individuals. One of them even testified that he himself was served by her."

"I don't know anything about that. I was concentrating on how I could help Dr. Peltz, who was getting sicker by the minute."

"Then I have to ask you," Cunningham continued. "How do you know that Dr. Peltz's dish was poisoned? And, even if it *was* poisoned, something with which we vehemently disagree, how would you know that it wasn't Martha Langston, for example, who put the poison in?"

"I don't know, … I just know it must have happened," replied Mrs. Feldman, now clearly flustered and agitated.

"So do you know what gastroenteritis is?"

No response.

"What about food poisoning, in the sense of contamination of the food by a microorganism?"

"I've had that. The symptoms start the day after the contaminated food is eaten—"

"Not at all," Cunningham interrupted. "Acute gastroenteritis caused by bacteria that produce their own toxins, like Staph or Clostridium, can cause extremely severe symptoms, just like the ones Dr. Peltz had, very quickly, definitely within no more than two or three hours after the contaminated food is eaten, sometimes even more quickly."

"One last question, if I may," Cunningham said. "Let's assume that your incredulous story, *fantastic* as it is, actually occurred. Why then would Dr. Rachel Moran, a gynecologist in Tallahassee, want to murder Dr. Peltz?"

"Well, … I don't know," she hesitated, "professional jealousy maybe, competition, or something very personal that occurred between them, ... I don't know. That's for you lawyers to find out."

"OK, again let's take the motives you listed seriously. Do you know how well Dr. Peltz and Dr. Moran knew each other?" Cunningham asked, knowing the answer too well.

"As I said, ... umm ... I don't know. But they were both doctors in the same region. They must have seen each other often at medical meetings, and, who knows, these encounters may well have become antagonistic."

"Mrs. Feldman, you may know and will hear later, that the defendant, Dr. Moran, saw Dr. Peltz only *twice*, since they have lived in Florida! *Twice!* And, on neither of those very brief occasions did they ever even *speak* with each other. Is that the kind of relationship, if you want to call it that, that might lead to premeditated murder?"

There was no response.

"I have no further questions, Your Honor."

Rachel continued to look enraged. The next witness called by the prosecution was Hunter Langston.

"Mr. Langston," Griffin began, "what has been your relationship with the victim, Dr. Peltz, and the defendant, Rachel Moran? And where do you currently reside?"

"Ah have been thuh housekeeper for Dr. Peltz for many years," Hunter replied.

"And in that capacity, what exactly do you do?"

"Wayul, Ah maintain thuh house in good shape, fix whatever iz broken, run whatever errands is needed, do general cleaning, mow thuh lawn, and the such."

"Have you had a good personal relationship with Dr. Peltz, Mr. Langston?"

"Very good. In fact, Dr. Peltz promised may thet hay would leave that whole estate tuh me after he died. He sayud hay didn't have no relatives, an' in sum ways ah wuz lahk uh son tuh him."

"Where do you live, Hunter? May I call you Hunter?"

"Dr. Peltz had uh log cabin built fahwar me on thuh edge uh thuh forest. It's naw more than fifty yards frum his house. Thet way, Ah can always keep an eye on it. Watch fahwar suspicious comings an' goings, an all thet."

"Anything else about that log cabin, Hunter?"

"Wayul, thuh cabin iz on top of uh hill thet looks down on thuh harbor whayer his private fishin' boat iz docked. Ah maintain thet too."

"And Rachel Moran?"

"Ah don't know much 'bout her. Shay izza good friend uh mah stepmah, Martha Langston. That's all. Have maybe sayn her gist uh couple uh tahms."

"Let me take you back to that night in April when Dr. Peltz was brought back to his home very ill after a seder feast. How were you involved?"

"Ah saw thuh comings an' goings of cars Ah had nevur sayn before. It looked lahk thayure wuz sum commotion bringing thuh doctor inside."

"So what did you do?"

"Ah waited an air or two an' then came ovur tuh thuh house tuh ask whut wuz happening. My Ma an' that Rachel woman, they wuz tawkin' in thuh livin' room … lahk as if thayure wuz nuthin' wrong. Then Ma pointed to thuh room whayer Dr. Peltz wuz lyin' in bed. Ah then Ah went in there."

"How did you find his condition?"

"Hay wuz very sick. Breathin' fast. Hay had soiled his trousers. But hay wuz awake an' tried tuh talk tuh me. Ah couldn't understaynd most uh whut he sayud. Hay handed may uh piece uh paper with thuh name and contact information of someone hay wanted may tuh call raht away. He told may whut Ah should say.

"What was the name on that paper. Do you recall?" Griffin asked.

"God, Ah just don't remember. Let may thank."

"Take your time," Griffin reassured Hunter.

"Bert ... Kru ... something."

"Herbert Krüger?"

"Yayus, that's it!" Hunter declared.

"So, Hunter, did you speak to Mr. Krüger?"

"Naw, hay wasn't thayure. But Ah talked with sum kinduh deputy or whatever and told him tuh find Mr. Kru ..."

"Krüger."

"Krüger. And give him thuh message frum Dr. Peltz as soon as possible. Hay sayud OK, raht away."

"Then what did you do, Hunter?"

"Ah just left tuh go home tuh party with mah friends, as we always do evur Friday night."

"All right. Did you see anything after you left Dr. Peltz's house?"

"Well, wheyun Ah stepped out later in thuh night to git sum fresh air, Ah saw two people carryin' uh bag toward thuh shore whayer the doctor's boat wuz docked."

"What kind of bag?"

"Uh big wun. Big enough tuh accommodate uh body—"

"Objection!" Chase Aiken sprung to his feet. "That's mere speculation, your Honor."

"Sustained. The jury will disregard that last statement. Go ahead, Mr. Langston."

"I couldn't make out who thuh two paypul wuz. Ah didn't see thur faces in thuh dark, even with thuh moonlight. But now I know. It must hav been mah Stepma an' Rachel."

"Objection!" Aiken jumped up again. "Pure speculation."

"Sustained. The jury will disregard that last statement also," Judge Rutledge said, this time clearly annoyed.

"One last question, if I may," said Griffin. "Did you ever encounter the defendant before that night?"

"Yeah, maybe a glance. But wait, now that yawl mention it. Late wun night Ah wuz walkin' around thuh house an' came upon her diggin' up something in thuh garden. Ah still don't know whut."

"Thank you, Mr. Langston, that's all I have," concluded Griffin.

36

The Corpse

Drew Griffin then called his last witness to the stand—Dr. Stewart Bradshaw, who had recently performed the autopsy of the body recovered from the beach.

"Dr. Bradshaw," Griffin began. "You performed the autopsy on Dr. Peltz, is that correct?"

"Yes, sir."

"Please tell the court your medical background and qualifications."

"I am an MD graduate of the University of Alabama medical school. After that, I did a three-year residency in pathology at Tallahassee Memorial Hospital. Pathologists are trained to do autopsies. I am certified by the American Board of Pathology," said Bradshaw.

"Can you tell us, please, doctor, how many autopsies you have yourself performed or participated in?"

"Well, I've lost count of that," Bradshaw replied. "I would say at least a couple of hundred. All of them at Tallahassee Memorial Hospital where I am in charge of anatomic pathology."

"Doctor Bradshaw, we have all read your final report of Dr. Peltz's postmortem exam. We're also aware of the limitations you had, caused by the lack of sophisticated tests at this time that can definitively and with certainty identify a dead body, ... especially in a drowning case. Can you comment on that, doctor?"

"The typical external appearance of a decedent who has drowned in a large body of water—" Bradshaw began.

"You mean like the Gulf of Mexico?" Griffin interrupted.

"Yes, sir. Their external appearance usually includes cyanotic bloating of the face and abdomen ... to the point of sometimes not being identifiable by relatives, widespread skin desquamation, and signs of all sorts of blunt force injuries and lacerations."

"How do you know then that these external injuries you described in your report weren't the result of assault or even murder of the victim *before* being drowned?" Griffin asked, knowing full well what the answer would be.

"Exactly," replied the pathologist. "Wounds could have been inflicted while still alive. *Or* the wounds could have been sustained *after* drowning. You would expect the drowned corpse to encounter and knock into rocks and other objects or to be dragged along the bottom surface with sharp surfaces floating in the water ... and animal predation can promote decomposition and profoundly obscure the decedent's external body landmarks," said Bradshaw.[40]

"Thank you, Doctor," concluded Griffin.

Chase Aiken practically jumped out of his seat to start the cross-examination.

"Dr. Bradshaw, you told us your qualifications as a pathologist. But have you had special training in *forensic* pathology?"

"Forensic pathology?" Bradshaw replied. "Well, yes, sir, we studied forensic pathology during our pathology residency."

"No, no," said Aiken, "I mean, are you *board certified* as a *forensic* pathologist? I believe that requires special, additional training in a fellowship to become a medical examiner."

"Well, sir, I haven't got that."

"So you are not an expert in autopsies, is that right, doctor?"

Drew Griffin stood up. "Objection, Your Honor. The witness has already explained that he is considered to be an expert in this part of Florida!"

"Sustained," declared Judge Rutledge.

"OK then, doctor, you concluded in your report that the recovered corpse was most likely to be that of Dr. Peltz. Given the general lack of advanced laboratory tests or other data to provide proof of identity, what led you to form that conclusion?"

"It was almost entirely the anthropometric information."

"Like height?" Aiken asked.

"Yes, exactly."

"He was five feet nine in height," replied Bradshaw, finding that in the report he held in his hands.

"I mean, like what was his *right side* height?"

"I don't know what you mean by right side, sir," replied Bradshaw, looking flustered.

"Well, doctor, did you measure his right and left leg lengths?

"Yes, of course, I measured it everywhere."

"So did you know, doctor," Aiken asked, "that Dr. Peltz walked with a very prominent limp? We asked many individuals who knew him. He had a congenital skeletal anomaly that made his left leg at least two inches shorter than his right one. And in these autopsy photographs you have provided," Aiken said, holding up the photographs, "I can't see any evidence ... any evidence at all ... of differences in leg lengths in this corpse. Can you?"

Aiken handed Dr. Bradshaw the photographs. He looked at them closely, turning them in all directions, at arm's length and close up to his eyes.

"I really don't see any difference in the legs," he finally said.

"Now, Dr. Bradshaw, did you see anything unusual about the hands of the corpse?"

"The hands?" Bradshaw asked.

"Yes, you know, these things," as Aiken held out his own hands, fingers spread.

"Well, no sir. His hands and fingers were bloated but otherwise completely normal."

"Well, Dr. Bradshaw, let me ask you if you knew from others that Dr. Peltz's left middle finger was missing, amputated below the middle knuckle, leaving only a stump. He told people that this was due to a childhood accident," said Aiken.

Silence followed the question.

"Dr. Bradshaw?" Aiken stepped closer to the witness stand.

Bradshaw had nothing to say.

"Thank you, Dr. Bradshaw," I have no further questions." Aiken walked back to his seat.

Griffin called Bert Krüger to the witness stand. His testimony and cross-examination were not too helpful. He related Dr. Peltz's friendship with his father, all the way back to university in Germany where they were both students. Since he moved to Florida, it seemed like every time Dr. Peltz talked with Bert's father, he brought up his fear of being murdered, specifically by drowning. After a while, Bert's father dismissed Dr. Peltz's fears and found them almost amusing. So when Dr. Peltz called Bert that night to ask him to order a coast guard boat to look for him in the Gulf, off the Apalachicola coast, Bert went ahead and did it. After all, he reminded himself that Dr. Peltz had saved his life. When questioned, Krüger went over the items found in his motorboat, which Peltz never used, thus indicating that Dr. Peltz must have been inside it at some point.

On cross-examination, Aiken asked Krüger only about the specific items that were found in the motorboat. But then he focused on the events of that night in the Gulf of Mexico.

"So, Mr. Krüger, tell us what you and your colleagues saw that night on the Gulf, to the best of your memory."

"Yes, of course. I wasn't there myself, but the following morning I did interrogate the two coast guard officers who were deployed. They themselves were at quite a distance from the fishing boat. They noticed that the fishermen were struggling over something with their nets."

"Did you or your colleagues find out what all that agitation was about?"

"They told me that next to their boat something was gliding under the water. It turned out to be Dr. Peltz. The fishermen were astonished that he could hold his breath for so long while swimming just below the water with so much speed and agility. They pulled his limp body out of the gulf and into their boat.

"How do you know it was Peltz?" Aiken asked.

"Well, given the circumstances and his brief phone conversation with me a few hours earlier, I couldn't imagine who else would be swimming like that in the Gulf in the middle of the night," replied Bert.

"Would it mean then that Dr. Peltz was alive at that point," Aiken pressed on.

"Yes, I guess, I suppose so," answered Bert.

"And what did the fishermen say they did with him after pulling him out of the water?

"The fishermen brought him onto shore and called for an ambulance, but they were told that it would be better for him to be flown right away to Pensacola Hospital. It was able to provide intensive care. A rescue helicopter arrived on site quite quickly, and we assumed all was going to be well afterward. They did say that he was in a very bad condition. His breathing was shallow and fast. He was apparently very confused and disoriented. He didn't know what had happened. And when asked about his identity, he didn't respond. I didn't think he would survive the night."

"Thank you, Lieutenant Krüger. The prosecution rests, Your Honor."

The bailiff, Travis Dawson, now burst into the courtroom, holding up and flapping a piece of paper for the judge. It was from the pharmacist, declaring that the white pill was unidentifiable. He loudly announced to the court that "the pill was nowhere to be found in the up-to-date United States Pharmacopeia (USP) or in the National Formulary, a compendium of all FDA-approved drugs!"

37

Rachel on the Witness Stand

Cunningham chose to have Rachel testify first, a move that was well thought out.

"Please identify yourself, your birthplace, citizenship, and occupation at this time," Cunningham started.

"My name is Dr. Rachel Moran. I am a practicing gynecologist in Tallahassee. My husband, David Moran, is a professor at Florida State University. I was born in Budapest, Hungary, and I am now a full citizen of the United States of America."

"Can you please tell us about your relationship with Dr. Peltz from the beginning?"

"Shortly after Dr. Peltz settled into his new mansion in Apalachicola, he hosted a series of Sunday brunches to which he invited interesting groups of people who lived thereabouts or in Tallahassee. My husband and I were on the invite list, and we spent a very nice day there. That's where I met Martha Langston, who would soon become a good friend."

"I am sorry to interrupt, Dr. Moran, but as far as you know, was the relationship between Dr. Peltz and Mrs. Langston personal as well as professional?" asked Cunningham.

"Strictly professional. She was his housekeeper at that time after she escaped from her horribly abusive, alcoholic husband, a member of the Klan, I may add. They lived in a rundown trailer park. At the brunch, I may have said a brief hello to Dr. Peltz, nothing more."

"When did you next see him, Dr. Moran?"

"My next and last encounter with Dr. Peltz, up to the time of the April seder, occurred at a tea party hosted by the widow of a famous composer and conductor who had also taught music at FSU. As we listened to recordings of his compositions, I could barely take my eyes off Dr. Peltz, who was sitting a few seats over from where my husband and I sat. I didn't exchange any words with him. But somehow, I knew that I had seen him somewhere before. I became viscerally sick and had to leave with my husband. It was only weeks later that I remembered. And I only wish I hadn't because it changed my life.

"Dr. Peltz's former wife, who was now living in New York, had told Martha about some correspondence her former husband had with a man named Hans Wilhelm König. König was likewise a physician. He was a classmate of Dr. Peltz in medical school in Germany before the war. We did some research on Dr. König, and the findings were chilling. We needed to look further."

"What do you mean, Dr. Moran?"

"We gained access to a private safe in Dr. Peltz's home office. And in the safe were files that contained personal letters and documents. Some were addressed to Dr. König from high-level officers of the Nazi German government. There was also a formal notice on Nazi letterhead directing

Dr. König to immediately go to Auschwitz in Poland, where he would take a position as a physician."

"Well, did you report to anybody how you gained access to those letters?" Cunningham asked.

"Certainly. To the FBI and local authorities that were already investigating Dr. Peltz's practice and his distribution of illicit drugs."

"What was the connection between Drs. Peltz and König?" Cunningham asked rhetorically.

"When letters from Peltz were arranged on the left side of a table and those from König on the right, in chronologic order, close examination revealed something incredible. The letters of each man were consistently typed on different kinds of stationary, which made sense. But when scrutinized with a magnifying glass, what appeared was that they *all* had the same slight idiosyncrasies that manual typewriters tended to have in the 1950s (like a slipped *k* or a smudged *o*). Both Peltz's *and* König's!"

"Lord have mercy!" Cunningham exclaimed in feigned disbelief, slapping his own forehead. Rachel had told him about this before the trial.

"We figured that there could be only one conclusion. Dr. Ernest Peltz and Dr. Hans Wilhelm König were in fact one and the same man. And Peltz had been typing all the letters but on different stationary for each of them," said Rachel.[44]

The people in the courtroom sat forward in their chairs, as did some of the jury members. Not a whisper could be heard.

"Dr. Moran, do you know what Dr. König did at Auschwitz?"

"Not in detail. But he experimented with women prisoners, testing barbaric electroshocks to their brains, from which many died. He also tested psychiatric drugs on these women that were manufactured at the nearby I. M. Farben and Bayer pharmaceutical plants," Rachel replied. "We now know that he profited greatly from these experiments."[44]

"So do we know what happened to Dr. König after the war?" Cunningham broke in.

"As far as I could find out from different sources, at first König vanished after the war, eluded arrest, and was never tried for being the war criminal that he was."

"And why, Dr. Moran, were you so upset at that tea party about seeing Dr. Peltz, I guess we can say now, alias Dr. König?"

Rachel now took out a handkerchief for the first time and continued in a quivering voice, sometimes pausing to collect herself.

"As much as I have tried to forget, I distinctly remember König from the Auschwitz-Birkenau concentration camp. My twin sister Rebecca and I were deported there in 1944. We were thirteen ... almost fourteen years old, and we were separated from our parents who we never again saw. As the cattle car trains pulled up to the stop inside the camp, all the Jewish prisoners who had been stuffed into them for the three- or four-day journey were quickly sorted by Nazi guards on the platform into two lines. There was a line for those deemed able to work. Those people were assigned to hard labor and allowed to live, at least for a while. Those who were unable to do so, mainly the elderly and children ... well, they were made to jog, single file in a line directly to the gas chambers. But then there was one man, ..."

Now Rachel, tears running down her cheeks, turned away from the courtroom for a moment so the people in the room didn't see it.

"Excuse me," she said.

Cunningham asked the judge for a brief recess to allow Rachel time to pull herself together, which was granted.

"One man," Rachel picked up again after the recess, "one gap-toothed, handsome man, smirking smugly in full Nazi uniform with polished boots ... he was there for the selections for only one reason. Standing bolt upright, in a military posture, it was Josef Mengele. I later learned that he was called the 'Angel of Death,' a German doctor who was obsessed with the study of twins and now wanted twin prisoners to experiment on.[45] He was given a special place on the train platform. As the cattle cars were opened, and Jewish prisoners spilled out, Nazi officers ran up and down the length of the train, shouting *"Zwillinge heraus!"*—I'll never forget it. *"Twins out and over here!"*. The twins were then taken to Mengele, who briefly examined them and made a decision with a flick of his hand or pointing the riding crop he used to orchestrate the selections."

Rachel stopped to wipe away her tears and take a deep breath.

"My sister and I were selected for research study," she said. "In my family, I was the only one who survived Auschwitz."

"Thank you, Dr. Moran. That will be all for now. But I may recall you to the witness stand later, after Mr. Griffin is through cross-examining you."

Strolling over to Rachel, head down, Griffin started by looking directly at Rachel.

"Well, Dr. Moran, I must admit your testimony shocked all of us. What a terribly sad story. Please accept my sympathy," he said in a charmingly slow Southern drawl, stretching out his vowels.

Rachel was quietly and inconspicuously sobbing through her handkerchief.

"I'm personally moved by your story, as I am sure the jury is likewise," Griffin turned to the jury, pointing to them with his arm out.

"Not that I don't believe it, mind you" Griffin continued, "I'm trying to do so. So please forgive me … if I may ask … what proof or at least evidence can you provide us?"

Cunningham rose to his feet. "Objection, Your Honor! What evidence could Dr. Moran possibly provide almost twenty years later, after somehow escaping so bravely from the largest death camp in the history of the world?"

Before Judge Rutledge could respond, Rachel interrupted.

"May I make a correction, Your Honor, to keep facts straight?" Rachel asked looking up to the judge.

"Of course; go ahead," Rutledge said. Cunningham looked perplexed. He thought he knew everything.

"I didn't actually *escape* from Auschwitz-Birkenau."

"Correction noted," said the judge.

"You asked me for proof. I think I have it." Rachel stood up and took off her jacket.

Travis Dawson, the bailiff, immediately rose from his seat. "You can't do that, Ma'am. You must stay seated."

Rachel sat back down with her jacket off, and now slowly rolled up the long sleeves of her blouse, stretching out one arm with her hand facing up.

"Look," she said turning away from the exposed arm she had extended out.

Both Griffin and Cunningham approached. On the forearm was a slightly fading and smudged but readable tattoo with untidy handwriting: "166825ZW." The judge asked to see it also. This was the way the Nazis branded concentration camp prisoners, as if they were cows, but Rachel remained silent.

"What is the "ZW" at the end?" Griffin asked.

"That's for *"zwillinge,"* … "twins," she said.

Once again, silence settled over the courtroom.

"Rebecca and I were taken by guards to the Wooden

Blocking 1 barrack where twins were kept for Dr. Mengele's so-called research. Early the first morning, we were taken to Barrack 15 where Mengele's well-equipped but cold laboratory was located. When we arrived, several of Mengele's assistants were already hard at work. And there were children of all ages and genders, shivering and quietly sitting on benches, completely naked. Two Nazi guards, leaning into each other, pointed at them with their hands hiding their mouths. I'll never forget those smirks. We spent all day being meticulously examined, with all sorts of measurements taken by the assistants. Height, weight, head circumference, length of nose, body habitus, body hair, and other measures of maturity, including genitalia. And more, fingerprints and sole prints, hearing and dental tests, eye color, and ears. Many tubes of blood were taken. Rebecca almost fainted. From some children, not us, spinal fluid was painfully drawn. We heard them cry. And we had to run to different barracks for these tests, naked in the freezing cold. The next day the tests continued. X-rays, photographs, and psychiatric examinations. We thought it would never end, but it did on the third day."

"So were the two of you ever harmed in any way?" Griffin asked.

Pretending not to hear that, Rachel continued.

"A few days later, we were taken together to a laboratory in the camp we had not seen before. On one wall was an orderly display of dozens of extracted human eyes. They were terrifying because they all seemed to be looking at us. I still sometimes see them in nightmares. Mengele was possessed, ... like a madman, with the twisted idea of finding a way to change eye colors, especially from dark irises to light blue ones that would re-create those of Hitler's image of the Aryan race.

"Rebecca and I were ordered to lie down on two cold tables separated a few feet apart. Someone was already working on Rebecca. My sister was visibly squirming. Then Mengele appeared, carrying a long needle attached to a large syringe. He filled the syringe with a blue liquid from a glass container. Saying only *"guten morgen,"* he bent down close to my face to find the injection site. Before he did it, another face suddenly appeared, peering down, also close to my face. I didn't know who he was. But now I know. It was Dr. König! Mengele and König exchanged *"guten morgens,"* and then got down to business.[44] The intraocular injections directly into our eyes were extremely painful and both of us screamed loudly and for a long time. Two nurses were holding us down during the injections.

"An hour later, both of us were completely blind. We only gradually regained our eyesight, but vision for both of us remained blurry, our eyes inflamed and suppurated, watering profusely, and with our eyelids sometimes stuck together."

"Thank you, Dr. Moran; that will be all for me," said Griffin, turning around to walk to his chair.

"But I am not finished, Your Honor," protested Rachel.

"Well, go ahead, but please be succinct, Doctor," Rutledge said.

"Not long after the eye experiments, the two of us were again brought to Mengele's laboratory. He was in a convivial mood. He told us not to worry about another experiment he wanted to do.

This time, it was a study of cross-injection of spinal fluids between the twins. We had to lie on our sides on the tables, with our backs to each other. Mengele did my spinal tap, which was terribly painful, and I caught a glance at König doing the spinal tap on Rebecca. The procedures were done simultaneously. The two Nazi doctors then exchanged the syringes filled with spinal fluid and injected them at the same sites of the first spinal taps into the other sister. Rebecca screamed, and I must have blacked out.

What I didn't know at the time was that the doctors had diabolically, intentionally contaminated the syringes with streptococcal bacteria. Within hours, both of us had a high fever, shaking chills, neck stiffness, and the worst headaches of our young lives. I was sicker than Rebecca. I must have lost consciousness because I don't remember anything that might have happened for the next couple of days."

Chase Aiken stood up. "Your Honor, how long will we have to listen to all this sad tale?"

Before the judge could respond, Cunningham rose and said in his sonorous baritone voice, "Until the court understands fully the relationship between Dr. Peltz (a.k.a. Dr. König) and Dr. Moran!" The judge nodded toward Rachel to continue.

"The next thing I recalled was lying on a bed in the infirmary and being moved to a strange room with its windows painted white. My sister was already there, lying on a table. She seemed to be in a somewhat better condition than I was, and she called out to me. Another doctor in a white coat, with his back to me, was hovering over Rebecca. Next to him was a surgical rolling case cart. On it was a set of injection needles and syringes, some instruments, and cotton balls. The same cart was rolled to my side later. An assistant came over to pour a yellowish-pink liquid from a bottle into a small bowl on the cart. I later learned that the liquid was phenol. The assistant then placed a towel over Rebecca's eyes, while the doctor drew up the phenol from the bowl into a large syringe with a long needle. With a swift motion, he thrust the needle into Rebecca's chest, between her ribs and directly into her heart ..." Rachel had to pause. "Within seconds, she was dead. Other assistants picked up her limp, naked body, took it to a door they opened, and threw it into what looked like a pile of other bodies, ... like a used piece of cloth.[44]

"Then Mengele came into the room with König, both wearing white coats, and came to my side. Mengele started the preparations. I was certain that I was going to die next, like my twin sister. But then a Nazi guard came running into the room, excitedly ordering Mengele to go immediately to the camp commander's office. Herr Rudolf Höss[46] wanted to see him *immediately* because some kind of crisis had developed. Mengele asked if he could finish his case, but the guard grabbed his arm and said it was out of the question; immediately means immediately. And out they went, leaving me with König, who was only there to learn the procedure.

"It was January 26, 1945, a date I'll never forget. And, for the rest of my life, I will carry the guilt of seeing my sister murdered while I survived.

"I never saw Mengele again. He didn't return to finish the job. After waiting for what seemed like an eternity, I was helped back to the barracks by a nurse. I was groggy and disoriented. It turned out that the crisis for which Mengele was ordered to see Höss was the news that the Soviet Red Army was on its way from neighboring Kraków to liberate Auschwitz. I didn't know, but by then, most of the Nazi officers had evacuated, leaving some SS guards with orders to kill as many of the remaining skeletal prisoners as they could. The Soviet soldiers entered the camp the next day."

At that point, Judge Rutledge called for a thirty-minute recess. When he returned, Rachel was still on the witness stand, and Drew Griffin resumed his cross-examination.

"Doctor," he started, "I think all of us in the courtroom

have been shocked and shaken by your story. It was horrific. And I can now believe all you said."

Rachel appeared a bit more relaxed.

"But let me ask you a *hypothetical*," he said. "You pleaded *not guilty*, and we have to accept that at this point. So let's now suppose that someone else, someone unrelated to this case but also a Holocaust survivor, had encountered Dr. König under similar circumstances. Then, many years later after settling into a comfortable and prosperous life in America, she encountered Dr. König again in these United States and murdered him as revenge for torturing and killing the survivor's sister. Would that act of revenge be justified?"

Holden Cunningham and Chase Aiken sprung to their feet simultaneously. Cunningham's face was turning red as he bellowed, "Objection, Your Honor! Objection! Objection! This is the most outrageous, disgraceful, absurd question I've ever heard, trying to intentionally lure the defendant at a vulnerable point in this trial into falsely suggesting that she was indeed guilty. This goes far beyond the line of legal ethical conduct!" He was shaking. "And furthermore, the term 'hypothetical' is *never* used in a criminal trial!"

"Objection *sustained*," the judge asserted in an angry tone, leaning forward. "The recorder will delete from the record *all* that last passage spoken by the prosecutor. And, *Mister* Griffin, I will not allow another stunt like this from you. If you do anything like this again, I will declare a mistrial. Do you, *sir*, understand me?" The words *mister* and *sir* were loudly emphasized with contempt.

"Yes, Your Honor," Griffin whimpered. "I do apologize to the witness and the court."

"Well, ... go ahead then if you really must, but be *very* careful!"

Griffin cautiously approached Rachel on the witness

stand, but before he could say anything, Rachel spoke, addressing the judge.

"Your Honor, I would like to respond to his last question, if I may," she said. Rutledge nodded his head.

"My answer to the attorney's question, his so-called 'hypothetical' as he put it, is no. I don't think the revenge motive by itself would sufficiently justify killing. If that was the *only* motive."

"The *only* motive?" Griffin asked, perplexed.

"In a case like your 'hypothetical,' there would have to be much more," Rachel said.

"*More*?" Griffin asked, now looking confused.

"Yes," said Rachel. "Let's say your 'hypothetical' man or woman was a doctor who, having eluded trial for war crimes, came to America and ... let's say settled here in this part of Florida and opened a medical practice under another name. And what if that doctor started again killing more people, the doctor's own patients, in fact. What if he continued the covert and twisted, diabolic CIA-sponsored testing of mind-altering drugs, research he had started in New York, without even consenting the patients? Wouldn't his hypothetical Auschwitz victim who was now living in the same area, having discovered this, want to do *everything* possible and as soon as possible to keep him from continuing to kill?"

Griffin was now speechless, and the judge looked at Rachel quizzically.

"I don't understand," Griffin finally said. "Please elaborate on *your* 'hypothetical' statement."

"Dr. König, alias Dr. Peltz, was engaged in dangerous experiments on his unknowing patients, testing new mind-altering, hallucinogenic drugs. Something he started doing in New York several years earlier in the form of clinical trials financed covertly by the federal government. Again, without telling his patients. Without getting consent from his new victims. We know of at least four of his patients dying from those drugs."

"Your Honor, may I approach?" Griffin asked.

Rutledge waved for him to come over and added, "Mr. Cunningham, would you also please approach?"

The three of them huddled and spoke animatedly, without the jury hearing the conversation. The only thing they may have heard was Griffin, appearing outraged, asking why "we have never heard any of this background on Dr. Peltz."

Rutledge leaned over his desk, half-standing, as far as he could, and instructed the attorneys to come to his chambers behind the courtroom immediately, and then he called out for recess for lunch.

In chambers, Griffin requested that the conference go "on the record." Cunningham agreed. The court reporter was called in. With the door closed, Griffin complained vigorously that the prosecution was never informed about the pending allegations regarding Dr. Peltz's misconduct. Cunningham argued that it was the prosecution's job to thoroughly investigate the alleged victim's personal and professional background. Judge Rutledge agreed. Without providing details, Cunningham now told Griffin that the doctor had lost his medical license to practice in Florida because of this. He said that this followed an FBI investigation that included charges of illegal trafficking of unlabeled drugs across state lines from an unregistered pharmacy in Maryland. And the FBI had also started to investigate the deaths of Dr. Peltz's patients. "This man was essentially a sadistic serial killer," Cunningham concluded.

38

Daylight

Martha was waiting in her car for Rachel and David outside the courthouse. News tends to spread quickly around this part of Florida, so word had already gotten out throughout the community that Rachel was found not guilty. Martha was thereby exonerated and wouldn't have to go on trial for aiding and abetting the crime. After all, there was now no crime for her to be considered Rachel's accomplice.

Rachel and her attorneys made their way through a phalanx of local and national newspaper and TV reporters who were waiting for her, jostling on the courthouse steps to stick microphones in her face. The case was riveting enough to have gained some national attention. Finally liberated from the mob, they went to Rachel and David's home to relax and have some drinks. The Wolff family, including Nick, Martha's son, Jimmy Langston, Hunter, her stepson, and Martha's sister, Louisa, were already there. David had called them to come over as soon as the trial ended. They all stood up from their garden chairs and applauded as Rachel approached. Martha had not been allowed entry into the courtroom during the trial to hear the testimonies and Rachel's cross-examination, in anticipation of her own trial to follow Rachel's *if* Rachel had been found guilty. So Martha now couldn't wait to hear the details.

Martha also had some good news to tell them. She now revealed to them for the first time that she had met a man of her age who was in her FSU class. He was a kind, intelligent, and quite well-to-do man with a sense of humor and wide interests he shared with her. He was a successful businessman outside the FSU classes who now wanted to go full time to law school. During this period, they had secretly fallen madly in love, and now Martha wanted to show her friends her sparkling engagement ring. Her friends and relatives stood up to take turns to warmly embrace her. Rachel kissed Martha with a big smile on her face over which tears streamed down to her cheeks. She was at a loss for words, so she just blabbered "I knew you would, … the day I met you."

Epilogue

In May 1964, Martha Langston graduated from FSU with a master of social work degree. Her inner circle of family and friends, her fiancée, and dozens of acquaintances and students whose lives she had touched were at the commencement ceremony, sitting together in a cluster with pride and in amazement of how far Martha had gotten with her life from an almost hopeless personal and social situation. And in August, Martha was invited to teach a class on poverty, oppression, segregation, and culture as determinants of social services provided to individuals and communities.

At almost the same time, an aging, frail man was awakening in his shabby, one-room apartment outside the small city of New Braunfels, Texas.[47] He slowly, clumsily got dressed, every now and then having to sit down on his worn, threadbare armchair to catch his breath. He then brewed some coffee for himself but spilled some of it, scalding his hand. Reflexively, he blurted out a profanity directed at nobody special. Fumbling without success to put on a bow tie with a missing finger, he finally threw it on the floor. As a country doctor, he worked in a dilapidated, stand-alone building close to his home. He used a rolling walker to go there and back, hunched over it under the blistering Texas sun. The clinic was not air-conditioned; only a couple of large ceiling fans provided some relief from the musty, airless oppressiveness of the waiting room. Several patients were already waiting. The receptionist, an old, grumpy, retired nurse, stood up when he entered.

"Dr. Krämer," she said scornfully, "you are more than a half hour late. Let's get going!"

She helped him put on a rumpled, stained white coat that was much too large for him. Still sweating from the walk in the heat, the cheerless old man stumbled with a conspicuous limp to call for his first patient with a heavy German accent.[48]

Notes and Citations

1. The first civil rights sit-in in the country took place in Wilmington, North Carolina, on February 1, 1960, at a Woolworth's store luncheon counter. The nonviolent protesters were arrested, but their action later prompted the F. W. Woolworth Company store chain to remove its policy of racial segregation in the South. This inspired the events in Tallahassee, a couple of weeks later, organized by the local chapter of the Congress for Racial Equality (CORE). The sit-ins there continued for several weeks, resulting in multiple student arrests, trials that found them guilty, and imprisonment for over a month in some cases. (From: https://history.fsu.edu/article/black-history-month-story-tallahassee-sit#).

2. The naturalist Gloria Jahoda authored a remarkably observant and elegantly written book vividly describing this part of Florida (Jahoda F. *The Other Florida*, New York: Charles Scribner's Sons, 1967). In 1895, a man named W. C. Tully founded the town of Panacea, Greek for "healing all,"

so named for the supposed curative powers of the mineral springs that were located in the area. By the early 1900s, tourists from around the country flocked to Panacea, carrying prescriptions from their doctors to recuperate in the medicinal properties of the cold, clear, and often odorous mineral springs of Panacea. At its peak, a luxury hotel was built there, named the Panacea Mineral Springs Hotel. ("It'll cure what ails ya!" "Florida Memory," State Library and Archives of Florida, November 11, 2014.) The hotel burned down in the 1920s, after which the Great Depression and hurricanes, followed by World War II, took a major toll on the community's economy. By the mid-twentieth century, the population had declined seriously. Today, there are more boats than cars in the town. Oyster shells line many of the roads, reflecting the town's coastal history. Today, there are only remnants of the concrete structures for six of the springs. Nestled between the St. Marks National Wildlife Refuge and the Apalachicola National Forest, the small town of Panacea is a prototypical "Old South" community.

3   The phrases "White trash" and "trailer trash" arose in the early 1950s as very demeaning terms for particularly poor White people living in trailers. Mostly in the South, such labels were also used along with "redneck." After World War II, poor Whites who couldn't purchase suburban housing began to buy mobile homes. They were not only much cheaper, but they could also be easily relocated by people living in them who had job opportunities elsewhere.

Harold H. Martin, *"Don't Call Them Trailer Trash,"* *Saturday Evening Post*, 225, no. 5, August 2, 1952.

Nancy Isenberg, *White Trash: The 400-year Untold History of Class in America*, New York: Penguin Books, 2016.

4   A Kleagle is an officer in the Ku Klux Klan whose responsibilities are to recruit new members and maintain control. The history of women in the Klan went through several periods. Hundreds of thousands of women poured into the "ladies" organization in the mid-1920s. However, this era collapsed rapidly. By 1939, only about fifty thousand women and men still belonged to the KKK. This was the result of conflicts among the leadership factions of the Klan, rampant corruption, and public discovery of atrocities committed by the Klan that seriously damaged its image. Between 1930 and 1945 the Klan was drastically reduced in numbers of both men and women, which were based mainly in the South. The roles of women in Klan activities diminished. The reemergence of the KKK in the 1950s was stimulated by national efforts to accelerate racial desegregation. The role of women reemerged in full force by the end of the 1950s, with women donning Klan robes and hoods.

Kathleen M. Blee, *Women of the Klan*. Berkeley: University of California Press, 2009.

5   Kristallnacht ("The Night of Broken Glass"), so called because of the shattered glass that afterward littered the streets following the . . . vandalism and destruction of Jewish-owned businesses, synagogues, and homes took place in Berlin and throughout Germany on November 9–10, 1938. These events were explicated by the Nazi Party as a "spontaneous outburst of public sentiment" in response to the assassination of a German diplomat in Paris by a seventeen-year-old Polish Jew two days earlier. Propaganda Minister Joseph Goebbels went further when he announced that "World Jewry" had conspired to commit the assassination. The rioters were mainly

"Brownshirts" (*Sturm Abeilung*), the paramilitary wing of the Nazi Party, and Hitler Youth. They destroyed or set on fire hundreds of synagogues and cemeteries, shattered the shop windows of about seventy-five hundred Jewish-owned commercial establishments and looted their wares throughout the night.

The Night of Broken Glass. Holocaust Encyclopedia. US Holocaust Memorial Museum, 2023. https://encyclopedia.ushmm.org

Martin Gilbert. *Kristallnacht: Prelude to Destruction.* New York: Harper Collins, 2006.

6 Anti-Jewish laws, deportations, violence, and even concentration camps were already in force at this time, but the Nazi Party wanted to present a much more sympathetic national face to the world. So Dr. Peltz was one of the few Jewish athletes who were permitted to participate in the 1936 Olympics.

7 Angelo's Seafood is a legendary establishment, still open in Panacea, having been run by five generations of a family. Constructed in 1945, the restaurant boomed from the start. By the summers of the 1950s, cars parked all the way from the water back to the intersection and overflowed into the lot of a nearby filling station. On July 10, 2005, Hurricane Denis irreparably damaged the building, which had to be demolished and rebuilt. The restaurant has always served fresh, local, boat-to-table seafood.

8 By this time the pseudoscience of eugenics was well established in Germany, based almost entirely on myth and conspiracy theories, leading to the Nuremberg laws and decrees, beginning in 1935, mandating the exclusion

of German Jews from entry into law schools, medical schools, and other professional institutions, and forbidding intermarriage across blood lines.

9 Stone, Dan. *The Holocaust: An Unfinished History.* UK: Pelican Books, Penguin Random House, 2023, 82.

10 The beautiful Degas of *Five Dancing Women* (Ballerinas) had been missing since around 1940, when Nazis stole it from Jewish Baron Mór Lipót Herzog's collection. ("After 75 Years and 15 Claims, a Bid to Regain Lost Art Inches Forward," *New York Times*, October 17, 2020.) (history collection.com) Stephanie Schoppert, *"10 Pieces of art stolen by the Nazis that are still missing today."* September 2016.

11 Ernő Dohnányi (1877–1960) was a world-renowned Hungarian composer, pianist, and conductor. After World War II, he and his wife emigrated to the United States, and they became US citizens in 1955. In 1949, the couple moved to Tallahassee, Florida, where the maestro taught for ten years at Florida State University's School of Music. His son, Christopher von Dohnányi, became the exceptional music director and conductor of the Cleveland Orchestra. Ernő Dohnányi performed in public for the last time on January 30, 1960, conducting the university orchestra in Beethoven's *Piano Concerto No. 9* with his doctoral student as piano soloist. Dohnányi died ten days later of pneumonia.

12 After the end of World War II, many prominent Nazis, including physicians and lawyers, were captured and tried as war criminals in Nuremberg, leading to long prison terms or execution. However, many also eluded capture and arrest. Initially, visas to America were precious

and few. Yet, Nazi collaborators and even SS members of Hitler's reign of persecution, men who proudly wore Nazi uniforms, were often able to enter the United States as "war refugees." Thousands of others were able to enter illegally. And hundreds more had covert help from secret military and intelligence officials at the Pentagon, the CIA, and other agencies. For many years, the Soviet Union and the United States competed vigorously during the Cold War to bring into their countries the best Nazi scientists, doctors, mathematicians, and engineers. In 2010, a secret history of our government's decades-long hunt for war criminals concluded that the United States became a refuge for the Nazis after World War II. The Justice Department stated that "America, which prided itself on being a safe haven for the persecuted, became ... a safe haven for the persecutors as well." Locations of Nazis pursued by the Office of Special Investigations were mainly concentrated in the Northeast, Midwest, and Florida, including five in the Tallahassee area. (Eric Lichtblau. *The Nazis Next Door: How America Became a Safe Haven for Hitler's Men.* Boston: Houghton Mifflin Harcourt, 2014. See map of locations on pages 232–33.)

Also:

Christopher Schiessl. *Alleged Nazi Collaborators in the United States after World War II.* Lanham: Lexington Books, 2016, and

Howard Blum. *Wanted! The Search for Nazis in America.* New York: Quadrangle/The New York Times Book Co., 1977.

13 Operation Paperclip was a postwar US intelligence program that brought Nazi German scientists to the United States under secret military contracts. American war crimes

investigators were sent into the field to locate German physicians, with the purpose of interrogating them. One of these investigators was Dr. Harold Abramson. Abramson would later become a central player in one of the most dramatic events in the history of Operation Paperclip. Later, the code name Operation Bluebird, subsequently renamed Operation Artichoke, split off to specialize in behavior modification programs. Also see citation 22.

Investigative journalism in the 1970s led to a series of hearings in the US House of Representatives, which concluded that American military leaders had made morally bankrupt decisions on the grounds of national security. As a result, the Justice Department opened the Office of Special Investigations (OSI).

14 http://en.wikipedia.org/wiki/Project_MKUltra; and The Church Senate Subcommittee, MKUltra: http://www.nytimes.com/packages/pdf/national/13inmate_ProjectMKULTRA.pdf.

15 Brozan N. "Out of Death, a Zest for Life," *New York Times*, Nov. 15, 1982, Section C, 20.

16 The Deep Creek Lake two-story house still stands today on Glendalock Lane, off Deep Creek Drive on an easy-to-miss gravel dead-end road, near US 219.

17 More recently, the Hotel Pennsylvania, across from Penn Station.

18 H. P. Albarelli Jr. *A Terrible Mistake. The Murder of Frank Olson and the CIA's Secret Cold War Experiments*. Walterville, OR: Trine Day LLC, 2009.

19. Kijakazi K, K. Smith, C. Runes. "African American Economic Security and the Role of Social Security," Washington, DC, Urban Institute, July 2019. www.urban.org.

20. The history of American medicine is appallingly stained by the exploitation of African Americans for unethical medical experimentation performed on these people without informed consent. The notorious Tuskegee Study ("Tuskegee Study of Untreated Syphilis in the Negro Male" supported by the United States Public Health Service) was conducted over a period of forty years (1932-1972) on over six hundred African American males with syphilis in Macon County, Alabama. These individuals were told they were being given medicine for "bad blood," yet in fact they were unwittingly given placebos. Although a penicillin cure for syphilis was widely available, the study was designed to "observe" the natural history of *untreated* syphilis, which can (and did) result in devastating long-term consequences such as painful ulcers, progressive paralysis, and neurologic disorders. Henrietta Lacks was an African American woman who was unsuccessfully treated for cervical cancer at Johns Hopkins University in 1951. Without her permission, she had her cancer cells taken out and grown in tissue cultures in a laboratory, where those cells (called HeLa cells) could infinitely multiply. Although these cells were subsequently invaluable for medical research around the world, a biotech company in the United States commercialized them for sale at enormous profits. Until quite recently, none of the family members of Henrietta Lacks even knew about this.

    The so-called "PolyHeme study" was done in the mid-twentieth century in two dozen cities around the

United States, where ambulance services in predominantly Black neighborhoods would be directed to bring African-Americans after severe trauma to local hospitals that were participating in the study. There, instead of being given real blood (red cells), they were given a substance called PolyHeme, an experimental oxygen-carrying substitute for red blood cells to see how effective it was: it wasn't. The patients and their families were never informed. See: Rebecca Skloot. *The Immortal Life of Henrietta Lacks*. 2010: New York: Crown Publishing, Random House; Harriet Washington. *Medical Apartheid. The Dark History of Medical Experimentation on Black Americans from Colonial Times to the Present*. 2006: New York: Harlem Moon Broadway Books; Scharff DP, Mathews KJ, Jackson P, at al. "More than Tuskegee: Understanding mistrust about research participation." J Health Care Poor Underserved 2010;21:879-897.

21 The role of women in the KKK changed over the years. In the first two iterations of the Klan, starting in 1871 and 1915, respectively, women did not participate except as auxiliaries, as social clubs, with women sewing and making clothes for their husbands, and playing a symbolic role to shield angelic female innocents from the terrifying Black "demons" who had been unleashed on the countryside. The second era saw the creation of the Women's KKK, an affiliated but separate organization specifically for White Protestant women. With very rare exceptions, the WKKK did not engage in lynching and other acts of violence with their male counterparts. WKKK members did, however, form so-called "poison squads," or whisper networks, to destroy the reputations of anti-Klan political candidates by claiming they were

Jewish or Catholic. In whatever capacity they served the Klan, women were regarded as second class to their husbands and other Klan males. It was only in its third era, into the 1960s in the South, that some women in the WKKK began to aid and abet their husbands in violent actions and spout racist and anti-Semitic rhetoric in public. WKKK members now wore full Klan regalia for meetings. (Emily Cataneo. "A Brief History of the Women's KKK," October 14, 2020. https://daily.jstor.org/daily-author/emily-cataneo/).

22 Also see citation 13. After the CIA was founded in 1947, Dr. Harold Abramson (November 27, 1899–September 29, 1980) became one of its first medical collaborators Abramson helped design early mind control experiments. He received his MD from Columbia College of Physicians & Surgeons in 1923, specializing in allergy medicine. He joined the staff of Mount Sinai Hospital in New York City in 1941, with expertise in asthma and pulmonary disease. He was simultaneously appointed associate professor of physiology at Columbia. During the 1950s, Abramson was involved in highly controversial LSD research conducted on unwitting subjects at Mount Sinai for the MKULTRA program that was funded by the CIA. He used LSD stock ordered from Sandoz pharmaceuticals, and later an unlimited supply that Sidney Gottlieb and Eli Lilly made available to him. He also had a lucrative private practice in Manhattan. (Stephen Kinzer. *Poisoner in Chief: Sidney Gottlieb and the CIA Search for Mind Control*. New York: St. Martin's Griffin, 2020.

23 The Wehrmacht was the combined armed services of the Third Reich, one of which was the navy ("Kriegsmarine").

24 So named in the 1950s and 1960s, PPLO or the Eaton agent, is now known as *Mycoplasma pneumoniae*, a species of bacteria that today cause up to 40 percent of community-acquired pneumonia in otherwise healthy people. It is now known that these bacteria have absent cell walls, so they are not visible under the microscope on slides routinely stained to spotlight microorganisms that do have cell walls and therefore take up the stain. They are also not susceptible to antibiotics that kill bacteria by blocking their ability to build a cell wall around themselves. Antibiotics that work in ways other than by inhibiting bacterial cell wall production are in fact effective in treating Mycoplasma: examples are macrolides (like azithromycin), tetracyclines (like doxycycline), and fluoroquinolones (like levofloxacin). Mycoplasma pneumonia is transmitted via respiratory droplets, causing relatively limited epidemics every few years.

25 Heinrich Himmler (1900–1945) had by this time risen to the rank of Reichsminister of the Interior, directly reporting to Adolf Hitler. He was the founder of the Einsatzgruppen and the creator of the Nazi extermination camps from which he directed the killing of some six million Jews and another million people of "undesirable ethnicity." He was considered by many to be the architect of the Holocaust.

26 The formal designation for the Auschwitz-Birkenau concentration camp, fifty kilometers southwest of Kraków in today's Poland.

27 "In the Matter of Josef Mengele. A Report to the Attorney General of the United States." US Department of Justice. October 1992. https://www.justice.gov). König himself

performed electroshock experiments on selected Jews in the camp. Many of them died in the process.

28 Colnrade is a village in the Lower Saxony region of northeast Germany, bordering on the North Sea. Its closest major cities are Bremen and Hannover.

29 In the autobiography of Eva Mozes Kor, who had been a victim of Dr. Mengele's inhumane twin experiments, along with her twin sister, she notes that "an entourage of eight people accompanied Mengele on his 'rounds,' and we later learned that the group included a doctor named König." Eva Mozes Kor: *Surviving the Angel of Death*, chapter 4. Indianapolis: Tanglewood Publishing, 2020.

30 Olga Lengyel. *Five Chimneys. A Woman Survivor's True Story of Auschwitz*. Chicago: Academy Chicago Publishers, originally Ziff-Davis Publishing, 1947. The book later became the inspiration for William Styron's award-winning novel, *Sophie's Choice*, later made into a movie starring Meryl Streep.

31 Czech H, Ungvari GS, Uzarczyk K, Weindling P, Gazday G. Electroconvulsive therapy in the shadow of the gas chambers. *Bulletin of the History of Medicine* 94, no. 2, Summer 2020. Johns Hopkins University Press.

32 The drugs being used (and their abbreviations or acronyms) were: LSD or lysergic acid diethylamide (LysAS-SDZ from Sandoz and LysAS-LIL from Eli Lilly), THC or tetrahydrocannabinol (Tetrahydrol), and psilocybin (PSILO). The "P" labeled pills were placebos. When the CIA was chartered in 1947, it was immediately interested

in testing drugs and plants or plant extracts for their potential to control minds (in competition with the Soviet Union). The so-called "Chemical Division" of the CIA was the authorized section of the agency charged with the investigation of chemical and biologic agent-induced alterations of the mind. The Chemical Division of the CIA was based at Fort Detrick, in Frederick, Maryland, where various temporary pharmacies were used as fronts for distribution to researchers. The flow of money from the CIA to support these scientists was established through charitable foundations like the Josiah P. Macy Foundation. A chemist named Sidney Gottlieb was recruited from Cal Tech to direct the Chemical Division. With the covert encouragement of Gottlieb, several secret operations were launched for research on mind-altering agents, including programs named MK-ULTRA and ARTICHOKE. (Jay Stevens. *Storming Heaven: LSD and the American Dream.* New York: Grove Press, 1987, 79–84.) In the case of LSD, the Swiss pharmaceutical company Sandoz had the patent for it. Sidney Gottlieb ordered the purchase of the entire inventory of LSD Sandoz had and then contracted for more. Concerned that a foreign source of LSD would not provide a reliable supply for the MK-ULTRA experiments, the program paid scientists at Eli Lilly, a domestic firm, to break the chemical code for LSD owned by Sandoz. They did so, enabling Eli Lilly to produce LSD in what it called tonnage quantities. (Stephen Kinzer. *Poisoner in Chief. Sidney Gottlieb and the CIA Search for Mind Control.* New York: St. Martin's Griffin, 2020, 74–107.) Much of the research was subcontracted (as so-called "subprojects") to outside institutions, including many renowned universities, hospitals, and medical schools throughout the United States As far as we know, practically none of these clinical studies underwent rigorous experimental planning, peer review, or oversight; nor did they follow consensus guidelines for the proper conduct of clinical trials. Study subjects were never asked for their consent and generally didn't even know they were being given psychotropic agents.

An Independent Commission of Experts was formed in 1996 by the Swiss government to probe Switzerland's wartime past. The commission singled out the Sandoz and Ciba pharmaceutical companies as important suppliers of drugs and chemicals for the Third Reich. While based in Switzerland, these companies owned factories in Germany from 1933 to 1945. Bayer and Hoechst emerged as the independent pharmaceutical giants that they are today following the mandated breakup of the IG Farben conglomerate after World War II. Remnants of their Nazi past included Fritz ter Meer, who was convicted of war crimes for his actions at Auschwitz, but was then elected to Bayer's executive board, a position he retained until 1964. (See IG Farben Trial) Independent Commission of Experts, https://www.uek.ch/en/auftrag/.

33 The Bureau of Narcotics and Dangerous Drugs was merged later in 1973 with the Office of Drug Abuse Law Enforcement to form today's US Drug Enforcement Administration (DEA), falling under the aegis of the US Department of Justice. The FBI was and is the investigative branch of the Department of Justice.

34 In Arthur Conan Doyle's short story titled "A Case of Identity," published in 1891, Sherlock Holmes identifies the false identity of a man who disappears by finding that his typewriter has the same idiosyncrasies of the

characters it types as the one belonging to his alter ego. Sherlock Holmes tells Dr. Watson: "It is a curious thing ... that a typewriter has really quite as much individuality as a man's handwriting. Unless they are quite new, no two of them write exactly alike. Some letters get more worn than others, and some wear only on one side."

35 Hans Wilhelm König evaded prosecution for his war crimes against humanity. He did in fact assume the pseudonym of Ernest Peltz. Klee, Ernst (1997). Auschwitz, die NS-Medizin und ihre Opfer. (In German) Fischer Verlag. ISBN 3-596-14906-1. Page 412. *Also see*: Hans Wilhelm König. Wikipedia https://de.wikipedia.org. and "Auschwitz doctor Hans Wilhelm König settled in a Lower Saxony village and practiced medicine as 'Ernst Peltz' before disappearing." In Introduction, page 17 (April 29, 2024) https://www.berghanbooks.com.

36 The beginning of a mourner's Kaddish, meaning "Glorified and sanctified be God's name throughout the world." The Mourner's Kaddish does not mention death at all, nor the name of the deceased, but instead praises God.

37 Oleander is one of the most popular shrubs in subtropical and tropical climates, particularly near seacoasts. It is commonly grown in Florida. All parts of the plant contain toxic glycosides that resemble the heart drug digitalis in action. Symptoms when ingested or even touched include nausea, vomiting, abdominal cramps, (Amy Stewart, *Wicked Plants*, Chapel Hill: Algonquin Books; 2009, 113–15.) diarrhea, dizziness, low pulse rate and irregular heartbeat, blurry vision, and eventually loss of consciousness and death. (Julia F. Morton, D.Sc.

Plants Poisonous to People in Florida and Other Warm Areas. Miami: Hallmark Press; 1995.) Because it is so widespread, it has been implicated in a surprising number of murders, suicides, and accidental deaths over the years. (Amy Stewart, et al. *Wicked Plants: The Weed That Killed Lincoln's Mother and Other Botanical Atrocities.* Chapel Hill: Algonquin Books, 2009).

38 Answering machines were already available at this time. The so-called *Ansafone* was being sold commercially by the Phonetel company in the United States since 1960.

39 "Direct evidence of Corpus Delicti." 61:740-744. *JSTOR* 1120202. Also, "People v. Leonard Ewing Scott." *JUSTIA US Law*, https:// law.justia.com/cases/California/court-of-appeal/2d/176/458.ht.

40 Caruso J. L. "Decomposition changes in bodies recovered from water," *Academic Forensic Pathology* 2016 no. 6:19–27.
Farrugia, A, B. Ludes. "Diagnostic of drowning in forensic medicine," chapter 3, *Forensic Medicine from Old Problems to New Challenges.* Duarte Nuno Vieria, ed. 2011.
Armstrong, E. J.; K. L. Erskine. "Investigation of drowning deaths: a practical review," Academic Forensic Pathology 2018; 8:8–43.

41 "Voire dire" is the process where lawyers ask potential jurors questions to determine whether they would be able to be impartial in the trial. "Peremptory strike" is different. It is a way for an attorney (for either the defense or the prosecution) to remove someone from the jury pool without having to show cause.

42 In general, all testimonies and conversations—anything said in the course of a trial—are recorded. This includes discussions that take place in the privacy of the judge's chambers. Juries can have access to all recordings, except those that take place in chambers. The rationale is that discussions with the judge in chambers relate to matters of law, but juries are charged with hearing only matters of fact, not legal nuances.

43 A Hebrew insult to describe a disgusting, revolting woman.

44 While assisting Mengele in his twin experiments, Hans König did his own studies on sick prisoners, testing their tolerance of new drugs not yet released on the market. Frequent effects on the prisoners included bloody vomiting, painful diarrhea, and lethal circulatory problems. In cases where the prisoners died, an autopsy was carried out to search for possible changes to internal organs. (Medical Experiments—Auschwitz, http://70.auschwitz.org). König worked with Dr. Josef Mengele in Auschwitz, assisting in making selections at the train stop for gas chambers.

Eva Mozes Kor mentions König, specifying that he was often with Mengele during the latter's experiments on twins. (Eva Mozes Kor and Lisa Rojany Buccieri, *Surviving the Angel of Death: The True Story of a Mengele Twin in Auschwitz*. Tanglewood Publishing distributed by Simon & Schuster, 2009).

After the war, it became known that König, *under the name of Ernest Peltz*, escaped to Colnrade, where he received a permit to practice medicine as a doctor from the British authority. When rumors about Peltz's authenticity began circulating and an investigation was opened, he closed his practice and fled the country, eluding trial for war crimes. While his whereabouts are unknown, it is believed that König (AKA Peltz) died around 1991. (Hans Wilhelm König, WIKIPEDIA)

45 These were experiments Josef Mengele did numerous times in Auschwitz, and they are well documented. Some children died afterward or died in gas chambers, so their eyes could be completely enucleated and either sent to Berlin for closer study by Mengele's mentor or displayed on his laboratory wall. The dye used was usually methylene blue but other substances may have been used also. Historically, there were no known children whose irises were changed in color for any length of time.

   Zegers RHC. The eye color experiment: from Berlin to Auschwitz and back. IMAJ 2020;22:219–23.

   Kor, Eva Mozes. *Surviving the Angel of Death*. Indianapolis: Tanglewood Publishing, 2020.

   Weindling, Paul. *Victims and Survivors of Nazi Human Experiments*, chapter 14, 157–65 (Jewish Twins). London: Bloomsbury, 2015.

   Langbein, H. *People in Auschwitz*, 336–42. Chapel Hill: University of North Carolina Press, 2004.

   Lifton, R. J. *The Nazi Doctors: Medical Killing and the Psychology of Genocide*, chapter 14: "Medical Killing with Syringes: Phenol Injections," ISBN 0-465-09094, 1986.

46 Rudolf Höss (also written Hoess) (25 Nov 1901–16 April 1947) was the notorious, longest-serving commandant of the Auschwitz concentration camp. He carried out the acceleration of Hitler's command for the extermination of the Jewish population of Nazi-occupied Europe, the

so-called "Final Solution." His sadism and, according to many, his apparent enjoyment of torturing and killing camp prisoners, has been captured in movies, most prominently *Schindler's List*, and, more recently, *The Zone of Interest*. After the war, he had the chutzpah, the gall, of writing his own perverted autobiography, which is a chilling book to read. (Rudolf Hoess. *Commandant of Auschwitz: The Autobiography of Rudolf Hoess*. London: Phoenix Press, 2000.) In his introduction to the book, Primo Levi (famous Italian-Jewish scientist, writer, and Holocaust survivor) stated: "The author comes across as what he was: a coarse, stupid, arrogant, long-winded scoundrel." After the war, Höss tried to hide under a false name with the aid of his family but was captured, tried for war crimes and crimes against humanity, convicted, and hanged in Poland in 1947.

47   New Braunfels, Texas, was a small city at that time, near San Antonio. It has been known for its German Texas heritage. It was established in the mid-nineteenth century by Prince Carl of Solms-Braunfels, commissioner general of the *Mainzer Adelsverein* (the Noblemen's Society). German immigrants settled there in large numbers, and by 1960 its population was 15,631.

48   Since the 1970s, the US government has initiated legal proceedings to expel only 137 of the estimated 10,000 suspected Nazi war criminals who found their way into the United States after World War II. Of the 137, twenty-eight died while their cases were pending. As of 2014, only ten suspects were ever prosecuted after being expelled or deported from the United States [Eric Lichtblau. *The Nazis Next Door*. Boston: Mariner Books, Houghton Mifflin

Harcourt, 2014. "Other suspected Nazi war criminals removed from the United States." The Associated Press, August 21, 2018. Rising, D; R. Herschaft, R. Lardner. Expelled Nazis paid millions in Social Security. AP, October 19, 2014.]

While most of the Nazi war criminals in the United States settled in the Northeast and Midwest, Florida was also a major destination for them. At least five were in Tallahassee. (Lichtblau, E., *The Nazis Next Door: How America Became a Safe Haven for Hitler's Men*. Boston: Mariner Books (an imprint of Harper Collins), 2014. See at the end of the book a map of the United States with locations of Nazis pursued by the Office of Special Investigations.)